## Praise for *The Cloths of Heaven*

'Graham Greene with a bit of Alexander McCall Smith
thrown in. Very readable, very humorous.
A charming first novel.'
*BBC Radio 5 Live*

'Populated by a cast of miscreants and misfits, this début
novel by playwright Eckstein is a darkly comic delight.'
*Choice*

'A fascinating novel – rich in dialogue with finely and
sensitively drawn characters. If you like Armistead Maupin,
Graham Greene or Barbara Trapido, you'll love this.'
*Bookgroup.info*

'A wonderful story. The picture of the diplomatic life is
spot on. The setting is a fictional part of West Africa but it's
so well realised that you feel as though you've been there.
It's a multi-stranded story with all the different threads
skilfully woven together. Splendid stuff.'
*The Bookbag*

'A wry, dust-dry character-observation-rich gem of a book
with one of the most refreshing comic voices I've read for a
long while. There are aspects of this book that I adored.
The playful tone. The wry observations. The brilliant
comic dialogue. And a cracking ending – both satisfying and
surprising. This book is a bright, witty companion – acute,
observant but also tolerant and understanding and not
afraid of a sharp jibe or two. If this book was a person,
I'd definitely invite it round to dinner. In fact, I might
even take it down the pub.'
*Vulpes Libris*

'A fantastically well executed novel. The book is a joy to
read. It is intriguing, exciting and just beautifully written.'
*Bookersatz*

'One of those brilliant books that offers an easy, entertaining read in the first instance, only to worm its way deeper into your mind. A modern Graham Greene – fabulous, fictional gold.'
*The Argus*

'A gripping new novel about ex-pat life in West Africa. A real treat.'
Brigid Keenan

'Marvellous on several levels. As good a page-turner as a thriller, with the lingering and satisfying afterglow of the best literary novels.'
Britain-Nigeria Educational Trust

'Well written, well observed and well nigh impossible to put down.'
Barbara Myers, *BBC Radio*

'Evocative, intriguing and with splashes of a modern Evelyn Waugh.'
Caroline Smailes

'I couldn't put this novel down. Eckstein's book will contribute to an important body of fiction written about the continuing relationship between African and European countries. Her background with VSO and now her work in medical ethics ensures that her perspective is informed, intelligent and demanding. This incisive intellect also delivers some fascinating, complex characters who won't necessarily behave the way you expect.'
Jackie Wills

'The scented evenings, heavily weighted with West African heat, seemed to rise from the pages as I read. I felt a slight sense of grief as the novel ended simply because it finished so perfectly and I wanted to spend more time in their world.'
*Chez Aspie*

*To read an extract from The Cloths of Heaven, turn to p.209*

## About the author

Sue Eckstein's first novel *The Cloths of Heaven* was published in 2009 and dramatised for BBC Radio 4's *Woman's Hour* in 2010. Her plays include *The Tuesday Group*, first performed in London in 2003, as well as *Kaffir Lilies*, *Laura* and *Old School Ties*, all for Radio 4.

# INTERPRETERS
## Sue Eckstein

Myriad Editions

First published in 2011 by

Myriad Editions
59 Lansdowne Place
Brighton BN3 1FL

www.MyriadEditions.com

1 3 5 7 9 10 8 6 4 2

A CIP catalogue record for this book is available
from the British Library.

ISBN: 978-0-9565599-6-8

Printed on FSC-accredited paper by
Cox & Wyman Limited, Reading, UK

*For Anna and Sebastian*

# relatively*speaking*

*In the third part of our series about people whose ways of living have challenged our definition of the family, Marcus Howe talks to Susanna Thomas and Max Rosenthal.*

SUSANNA THOMAS, 26, spent her early childhood in rural West Africa with her mother, anthropologist Dr Julia Rosenthal, before choosing to come back to England aged 11 to live with her uncle, Max Rosenthal. She now runs a batik business in London.

MAX ROSENTHAL, 53, is a Steiner school teacher and artist who has lived in communities in the West Country for nearly 30 years. During the past 20 years he has cared for over 35 foster children and young adults at risk.

## Susanna Thomas:

THE FIRST time that I remember meeting my uncle Max, I was about four and we'd flown back to England so my mother could go to a conference. It was the middle of winter and freezing cold. I remember watching him out of the window, skipping with his pupils. I should have been out there but I was wearing a pair of really cosy blue pyjamas that Max had bought for me which I liked so much that I wouldn't take them off, and it was too cold outside for pyjamas. My mum was standing out there with him, bundled up in one of his old jackets, laughing. I remember looking at Max surrounded by all those children

> 66 **When my mother refused to let me go, I decided to starve myself to death.** 99

and I just so wanted to be a part of it all.

In lots of ways, my first ten years living in Cameroon were quite idyllic. A mother who was always there for me. To whom I could tell absolutely anything. Who loved me more than anything or anyone in the world. And no school, no homework. I must have really hurt my mum when I told her I wanted to go back to England and live with Max, not just stay with him from time to time. She'd done everything she could to give me a fantastic childhood – the perfect childhood really – and all I wanted to do was get away from her. Not her exactly,

1

but that intense relationship where everything was always out in the open, where it always seemed there was nothing we didn't know about each other.

When my mother refused to let me go, I stopped eating. I decided to starve myself to death. I was only about ten or eleven but I was pretty stubborn and in the end she gave in. It's funny what children think of as normal. I never thought my life in Africa with my mother was particularly unusual. Nor Max's various set-ups in Dorset. And for a long time I thought everyone's grandmother was like mine. She comes across as a very normal, rather reserved elderly lady. But what a traveller!

*Continued overleaf* >

# Chapter One

I think I was about six when my mother tried to kill me, though I didn't know it at the time. It was probably somewhere around here – where the privet hedges give way to barriers of leylandii and high wrought-iron gates. I don't suppose it had anything to do with the hedges and gates, though they can't have helped. This place could induce a yearning for death in even the most optimistic.

To be fair to my mother, it wasn't me she wanted to kill. But she wasn't going to kill herself and leave my brother and me behind. I'm sure she would have succeeded at her attempt at oblivion, she was very good at whatever she did, except she hadn't anticipated my brother refusing to get in the car with her to fetch me from my friend Jackie's house. And she couldn't kill herself because she couldn't leave one of us behind. So here I am. Forty-five years later.

'So why *didn't* you get in the car?' I asked Max once. 'You were the good child. Obedient. You liked to please people. You must have known she was planning to do something terrible.'

'I can't remember anything much from that time, Julia. And anyway, what's the point in going over all that?'

'But you do remember you used to sleep in your cupboard,' I persisted. 'Curled up on the top shelf. With your little white blanket.'

'So?'

'Well, do you think sleeping in cupboards is particularly normal behaviour for an eight-year-old?'

'Who's talking about normal? What was ever normal? The cupboard just felt like a nice, safe place to be. More people should try it.'

Did *I* guess what she was trying to do? I don't think so. I remember her sitting in the kitchen with Jackie's parents. I think she was crying. I remember that they shut the door and wouldn't let us in. And that Jackie's father drove in front of our car, very slowly, all the way home.

The next day when I came back from school my mother had gone.

I'm getting closer now. Finally there is something I recognise. A pair of mock-Tudor mansions set high above the road, their lush front gardens – planned to the last designer shrub and exotic tree – sweeping down to the pavement. In one of the gardens there is a massive pond. Koi carp can live for years. I wonder if they remember the time, perhaps about thirty-five years ago, when the owner of one of the houses hired a helicopter and flew over the next-door garden. Then, having circled above it a number of times until his neighbour came out to see what was going on, he aimed a hunting rifle at the neighbour's head and shot him dead. That's what happens around here if you annoy people by erecting concrete nymphs and dryads and spotlights and fairy-lights, thereby detracting from your neighbour's ornamental pond.

Actually, it doesn't. That was the only time anything remotely like that happened during my childhood, but, whenever I passed these houses after that, I'd keep a good lookout for low-flying aircraft. I think the whole event was considered a little vulgar – both the erecting of the classical antiquities in the first place and the assassination of the householder who was guilty of such bad taste. I see that whoever lives here now has removed the statuary. The fashion seems to be more for bamboo. Less irritating altogether.

I indicate left at the end of the road and head south. I am aware that I am driving very, very slowly. The person in the car behind me keeps edging out, flashing his headlights, trying to overtake, but I can't seem to go any faster. The more familiar the streets and houses, the shops and churches become, the more I want to stop and go back. I pull up abruptly outside a church hall. The driver sounds his horn and passes me, screaming, 'Cunt!' as he does so. A group of pensioners look up in surprise. I'm a little surprised too.

Strangely, it was here, outside the church hall where I came to Brownies on Monday evenings, that I first heard the C-word from the boys hovering around outside, waiting for the infinitely more alluring Guides to arrive. When I was about eight, probably. And *rape*. A word that Caroline Statham – fellow Brownie and fount of all essential knowledge, particularly pertaining to the facts of life – told me meant having wire coat hangers stuck up your bottom. Something that would inevitably happen to you if you ever ventured off the open common land opposite her house and into the gorse bushes that harboured gangs of crouching, wire-wielding deviants. It was years before I learned the real meaning of the word, but it kept us out of the undergrowth.

I get out of the car and follow the elderly women into the church hall. I breathe in the familiar smell of damp wood, sweaty plimsolls and disinfectant. I wonder if the plaster of Paris toadstool is still in the cupboard next to the upright piano. Do eight-year-olds still dance around such things? I can't imagine it, somehow. Like those yellow scarves you had to spread out on the floor to fold in a particularly complicated way, it'll have been replaced with something altogether more practical. Some sort of fibreglass homage to world peace and multicultural harmony. Is that something else Susanna holds against me: a Brownie-free childhood? I wonder if Brown Owl remembered a Brownie with long fair plaits, very skinny legs and sticking-out teeth. An enthusiastic member of the Little People – a Sixer, no less. There's only one thing I remember about Brown Owl, apart from her tightly permed grey hair and fat calves – how she humiliated me in front of the whole pack when I listed the foods one might find on a well-stocked English breakfast table.

'Don't be ridiculous! No one eats *cheese* for breakfast!' she shrilled, her grey curls quivering with indignation. 'Tawny Owl! Did you see what Julia Rosenthal put on her breakfast list? Cheese! I *ask* you!' And, with that, my coveted Homemaker badge was left to languish in the box in the toadstool cupboard.

Brown Owl must be long dead so I should forgive her. But I don't. Nor, for that matter, Miss Pearson, the nursery school teacher I had when I was four, who made everyone on my table look at the way I held my knife and fork, and then told me to behave like a big girl and eat properly. Even now I can't do that thing where you mash bits of food on to the back of your fork. And I rarely eat peas. At least not in public.

'Can I help you?' one of the women asks. 'Are you interested in signing up for our Friday Crafts Club? We're always on the lookout for a bit of young blood. You'd be most welcome to join us.'

'Thanks,' I say. 'But I was just passing and wanted to see what this place looked like. I used to come here to Brownies. *Years* ago. In about 1967.'

'Well, I never! You'll know Margaret, then. Margaret! You'll never guess! One of your old Brownies is here to see you.'

And there she is – over by the piano. Brown Owl. Not dead at all. Taking a plastic bag of brightly coloured knitting wool out of the toadstool cupboard.

As I leave and head back to the car, I hear someone say, 'Well, she was here a minute ago, Margaret. How very strange.'

It's funny, the things you don't forgive. It's not the big things like your father drinking a bottle of whisky a night and walking into doors, or your best friend getting off with Nigel Blenkinsop in the fourth year at the St Peter's School Disco when she knew perfectly well that you really fancied him and had done for months. Or your daughter telling the whole world that the person she loved most as she was growing up was not you; that it was a kind of life entirely different from the one you had created for her that she'd craved.

It's the little things. Like being made to unpick the zip your mother had helped you to sew in for your handwork homework. I cried then. The only time I ever cried at school. I cried out of humiliation, not grief; because my mother had sewn it in for me beautifully, 'but not the way we do it here'.

Or maybe it wasn't humiliation. Maybe, I think now as I sit in the car outside the church hall, it was failure that made me cry. Failure to protect my mother from a hostile world which didn't recognise that she tried her best. Because she did. Whatever she did, she did as well as she possibly could, including being a mother. I wonder how many hundreds of miles she must have driven over the years, taking us to swimming lessons, skating lessons, music lessons – anything we wanted to do, she found a class, a teacher, a way of getting us there, a way of persuading my father to pay. Anything we became interested in, she bought us books or equipment for and never commented when we gave things up. When Max left his violin on the train, she drove to every station on the line to see if it had been handed in – which it hadn't. And then she somehow managed to buy him a new one.

Of course, at the time, I didn't appreciate any of that. I think that what I wanted more than any of those activities was an evening at home, all of us together, watching one of those old black and white films on TV or something, my parents sitting side by side on the sofa, looking happy. But that never happened. Not once.

My mother expressed her love for my brother and me in actions, definitely not in words and rarely in gestures, and so

7

we seldom sat still. I remember – it must have been around the time of the moon landing – asking my mother what would happen if Max and I went to live on the moon – how would she visit us? This was a quite a worry for us, as we knew how much she hated heights and flying. And she said she'd visit us *wherever* we went to live, even if it was on the moon. And we knew she meant it and we knew then how much she loved us. I don't think I've ever felt more loved than at that moment.

It's hard to hate someone whom you know would literally go beyond the ends of the earth for you without feeling like a traitor. And that's what I felt like all those times during my teenage years that I hated her – a traitor, a deserter. And then I hated her even more for making me feel like that. I wanted pure untainted hatred – the kind of straightforward, uncomplicated, cold hatred that most of my friends felt for their mothers – without the devastating guilt.

We went to Sunday School here too, Max and I. I remember, on our first day, Max carefully spelling out our surname to the elderly man in rather tight trousers who introduced himself as 'Mr-T-in-charge-of-under-sevens'.

'Are you sure that's right?' asked Mr T, squinting down at what he'd written in the register.

'Yes, R-O-S-E-N – '

'No, sorry, don't worry. I've got it,' he interrupted, flustered. I thought it was probably his trousers that were making him feel a bit uncomfortable. 'Go through to Miss Everett's class, Max. You're going to be making simply gorgeous collages of the Garden of Eden today, I believe. We've just had a new consignment of pipe-cleaners that'll be perfect for the serpents. And the crêpe paper! All the colours of the rainbow, and more besides. And you come with me, little Miss R. It's finger-painting for us. Joseph's coat is going to be the talk of the town. Danny La Rue will be spitting with envy.'

I didn't know who this Danny person was, but I felt rather sorry for him nevertheless.

I wonder why we went to Sunday School. I once found our baptism certificates while rummaging through a drawer in my father's study, but I don't remember either of my parents ever expressing an opinion about religion. I suppose we must have wanted to go, even though, for about a year, I used to cry until I was allowed to go into Max's class, where I'd sit very close to him, cross-legged, my fingers creeping towards his leg until I felt his warm, comforting skin. He never minded, but I got the impression that Mr T was rather hurt by my refusal to remain in his class of happy under-sevens.

Despite my accumulation of all the gospels for good attendance, God lost His appeal when Miss Everett gave us some sweet william seeds and a yoghurt pot ready-filled with potting compost.

'That's right, children, press the seeds right into the earth and then cover the top of the pot with the see-through plastic and put an elastic band round it. Max – help your sister, can you? There's compost going absolutely everywhere. There! That's lovely. Good boy, Max. Now all you have to do, children, is watch and see how God will make the seeds grow from the earth. *For it is fed and watered by God's almighty hand*, isn't it, children?'

By the next day, there was no sign whatsoever of God's greatness so I threw the pot away and embraced atheism, to which, apart from a brief flurry of religious fervour in my early teens, I have held ever since. I don't know if my brother believed in God then. I don't think he did, even though his patience resulted in an irritatingly impressive crop of deep red and purple flowers. And I don't know if he does now – though now he seems to be quite comfortable with all the tree-hugging and saint-veneration that goes on at his Steiner school in deepest Dorset.

I sit in the car and watch a parking attendant as he walks slowly up and down the road, checking out his reflection in the shop windows, adjusting his cap and tie, looking at his watch. I glance at the clock on the dashboard. My appointment isn't until four-thirty. I woke up before dawn this morning with Susanna's words dancing round and round in my head and a wisp of a dream of her and Max playing strange, dissonant sounds in front of a huge orchestra of faceless musicians. I got out of bed and went and sat in the garden watching the sky lighten, then got dressed, packed my bag and set off. And now I've mistimed my day so badly that I have several hours to kill and nowhere to go.

'Look, it's no big deal,' Max said on the phone the day the piece came out.

'Not for you, perhaps,' I said. 'It is for me. A massive great deal.'

'It hardly says anything about you.'

'Well, maybe that's the point.'

'What's the point?'

'That it hardly says anything about me.'

'But it's not about you. It's about Susanna and me.'

'Well, that makes it *so* much better.'

'Come on, Julia. It's called *Relatively Speaking*. It's not called *Mothers and Daughters Speak to the Nation about their Relationship with Each Other*. The journalist was looking for unusual families – stories about people choosing different ways of living.'

'Susanna could've chosen *me*. I chose a different way of living, didn't I? All those years we lived in Africa. Just her and me?'

'But she didn't. Maybe because she didn't feel she had to. Because you brought her up to be her own person, who makes her own decisions without worrying about what anyone else thinks of them. She didn't need to agonise about upsetting you, because she knows how strong you are. That's a good thing, isn't it? You can't have it both ways. Though that's never stopped you from trying.'

'But what do you think it looks like? That Susanna's most significant influence is her *uncle*. Not her mother.'

'That's not true, and, even if it was, what's so bad about that?'

'You'd know if you'd had children.'

'I have had children,' said Max quietly. 'Lots of them.'

If I were to get out of the car and walk past the row of shops where the parking attendant is still lingering, I'd pass the church where the gap-toothed vicar used to smile down at the Brownies and Cubs on church parade and hand out daffodils for us to take home on Mothering Sunday. I'd get to the privet hedges where Max and I used to pick food for our stick insects as we dawdled home for Sunday lunch. Amazingly, there's still a farm here, its entrance at the far end of the shopping parade. We came here on a Sunday School outing once and were made to sing hymns in the fields. The farm labourers stood leaning on their rakes and pitchforks, smiling in a slightly embarrassed way as we sang 'All Things Bright and Beautiful', Mr-T-in-charge-of-under-sevens' joyful contralto carrying in the autumn breeze. I feel my ears reddening just thinking about it. I should put some money in the parking meter. I should walk through those fields again now. Walk fast for a couple of hours until I feel better. But I don't get out of the car. I fumble in the glove compartment for one of the compilation cassettes that Susanna made me, years ago. *Happy Birthday, Mum*, it says on the label in her teenage handwriting. *I love you. Hope you love this*. There is a little heart above the *i*. I push the cassette into the player, then pull away from the church and set off towards our old house.

# I

(LONG SILENCE)

*So?*

So what?

*Shall we begin?*

Begin where?

*Anywhere you like.*

Is that all you're going to say?

*For now.*

And is that supposed to be helpful?

*I hope so.*

I don't know where to begin.

*You'll know. Just take your time.*

You would say that. Time is money. Isn't that the expression?

*Just take your time.*

(SILENCE)

I don't know where to begin. You'll have to give me some kind of clue. Some idea. Or is that against the rules?

*There aren't those sorts of rules.*

That's what you say.

*Well, what about beginning with a memory? Your earliest memory, perhaps.*

What are you expecting? Me floating about in the womb? The swish of warm amniotic fluid? The reassuring sound of my mother's heartbeat? The feeling of utter calm before the storm of birth? Isn't that the kind of thing you people are interested in? Or some kind of strange recurring dream in which I kill my mother and sleep with my father?

*I don't think we need be that ambitious.*

Do you think this is funny?

*Not at all. Do you?*

Do I look as though I think it's funny?

*No. You look rather sad. Are you sad?*

No more than usual.

*So. Let's start again, shall we?*

If you like.

*No, if **you** like. You can lie down if you'd prefer to.*

No, thank you. Sitting is fine.

*Right, then.*

I've told you. I don't know where to begin – what you want to hear.

*I want to hear what you want to tell me.*

I don't want to tell you anything.

*I don't think that's really the case. Is it?*

(LONG SILENCE)

*What is your earliest memory?*

I don't know.

*There's no hurry.*

Look, this is all a mistake. I've made a stupid mistake. Let's just stop now. Turn that thing off. Go on. Press the off switch.

*Are you sure you want me to?*

I don't know. No. Just leave it.

*All right.*

(LONG SILENCE)

Leaving Holland. That was probably it. My first real memory. Will that do?

*Go on.*

It was 1932. May 1932. If you're interested in those kinds of details. Are you?

*Go on.*

I was five years old and it felt like a great adventure, going on a long train journey with my mother. Is that the kind of thing?

*Go on. You're doing really well.*

I'd really rather you didn't patronise me.

*I'm not. I'm sorry if I gave you that impression.*

Have you any idea how hard this is for me?

*I think I have some understanding. I hope I do.*

This isn't something I'm used to.

*Not all that many people are.*

I don't mean paying to see someone. I mean talking. About myself. About my life. I'm finding it incredibly difficult. Talking. It isn't something I do.

*I know. It'll be hard. Just start and see what happens. See where your memories take you. Tell me about that journey. With your mother.*

It's really not that interesting.

*It doesn't have to be.*

So you're bored already?

*That's not what I said. Tell me about that journey.*

I don't think I'd been outside Amsterdam before. Yes, maybe once, to the seaside. And once or twice to my grandparents – my mother's parents – on the border.

*Yes...*

Yes what?

*Nothing. I'm listening. Go on.*

I remember I'd fallen asleep on the train with my head in my mother's lap and when I woke up there was a deep mark on my cheek – here – where the clip of her suspender had dug into me.

(SILENCE)

Are you sure that this is the kind of thing you want to hear?

*It's not what I want to hear. It's what you want to tell me.*

I don't want to tell you anything.

*But you came to see me. I'm right in thinking that no one forced you to come? There was no coercion?*

No one even knows I'm here. No one will ever know I've been here. But it doesn't mean I want to tell you anything.

*In your own time.*

I can't remember where I was.

*Waking up on the train. With your mother.*

Well, then, when we arrived in Berlin – the train was early – my mother told me to wait by the bags and went off to look for a porter. So I sat down on the biggest suitcase. I remember wondering why we'd brought so much luggage when we'd be going back to Amsterdam in the morning. I could still feel the mark on my cheek – like a little cave. I remember thinking it was like a little bear-cave. But you don't need to read anything particularly Freudian into that.

*I wasn't going to.*

And a man in a uniform with a whistle round his neck came up and asked me something but I couldn't understand what he was saying. It wasn't Dutch, though, I was sure. So I shrugged my shoulders and smiled and he went away.

(LONG SILENCE)

*And then what happened?*

I just sat there on the suitcase and after a little while I noticed a tall man waiting under the station clock. He looked terribly smart. He was wearing one of those hats – a trilby, you call them, don't you? – and a long, dark brown coat. I remember it very clearly. That lovely cashmere coat. He had his arm around a young woman's shoulders.

*Mmm.*

What?

*Go on.*

She had white-blonde curls – just like the ones I'd always wanted. My hair was dead straight whatever my mother did to it. I watched him and he looked up at the clock and said something to the woman. I can see it now, how he tipped her face up towards his – his hand under her chin like this – and kissed her on the lips and off she walked and I thought – how can anyone walk so elegantly in such high heels? And then he looked at me, this man in the hat and the beautiful coat – I don't think he'd seen me until that moment – and then he looked up again at the station clock. And suddenly there was my mother coming towards us with a porter pushing a trolley, and the man in the trilby looked at her and then nodded in my direction and said – I remember it so clearly – '*So! Hier ist der kleine Käse-Kopf.*' Do you speak German?

*I don't, I'm afraid.*

That's what he said: '*Hier ist der kleine Käse-Kopf.*' And he said it with a sort of smile so that for months – for months – I thought he had said something very nice about me.

*What **had** he said?*

It means 'little cheese head'. What? What's the matter?

*Nothing. You laughed.*

Did I? I can't think why.

*Carry on.*

My mother said, 'Shake hands with your father.' And I thought – what father? I don't have a father.

*Did you think he was dead?*

17

I don't think I'd ever given it a moment's thought. I was perfectly happy with my mother. I really don't think I ever wondered if I even had a father.

*You never wondered if you had a father?*

No. Is that so very terrible?

*Not at all. Carry on.*

It seems that, one day, he just wrote and sent for us. And so we went.

*And why do you think he sent for you?*

I haven't got a clue. I asked my mother – much later, of course – but she didn't seem to know any more than me. Or at least she didn't want to discuss it.

*Where had they met?*

Is that important?

*I just wondered.*

In Amsterdam. So my mother told me. When he was working there for some German engineering company and she was teaching in a school nearby.

*And they married?*

They did.

*And then what happened?*

He went back to Germany shortly before I was born and had nothing more to do with us.

*Why was that?*

I've no idea.

*Did your mother never discuss it? Later on?*

I don't think so.

*Did he support you?*

He might have sent my mother money, but I don't know if he did. I never found out why he changed his mind and sent for us. Maybe he was fed up with living on his own. A wife was probably cheaper than a housekeeper. Maybe he didn't want a Dutch child – a Dutch wife was bad enough – so he wanted me to grow up German. I don't know. And so there I was in Berlin – a cheese head.

*And how did you feel? About suddenly coming to Berlin?*

Feel? I don't know. But I was sure everything would be all right in the end. I was sure that my mother would take me home again very soon once we'd spent a day or two with this man she called my father.

# Chapter Two

Eynsford Park Estate is a tribute to the architectural glory of the 1960s, whose designers favoured the style of building most small children will produce if prevailed upon to draw a house. All that is missing are the sun's rays and the little black 'm's flying joyfully in the sky. When we moved here from a hospital flat in Bloomsbury the cement was still drying; the white paint on the timber cladding still gleamed; the newly seeded grass was only just beginning to clothe the bald verges. Our house, in Tenterden Close, was one of eight built round a circular green. For my mother it was like living in a Sartre play – only one way in and no way out. For us – for Max and me – it was heaven.

The first thing I notice as I drive into the cul-de-sac are the trees. On the green are three mature silver birches. For a moment I wonder how and when they got there. Then I realise that they are the saplings that used to serve us so well as rounders posts, as home in our games of 'It', as poles to grab on to and swing round and round until, too dizzy to stand up, we would collapse, shrieking with laughter, on to the grass. The trees are only a couple of years younger than I am. They have aged rather better.

I pull up outside number four, eject the cassette and switch off the engine. I sit in the car and look at the back door which, as with all the identical houses round the green, is at the side of the house. And I see the six-year-old me going up to it. In her school uniform – grey skirt, white shirt, maroon cardigan, grey and maroon striped tie, grey felt hat. She tries to open the door but it is locked. It is never locked. She knocks. After a while the door is opened by the woman who cleans for us once a week.

It's odd – I haven't thought about that woman for decades. Mrs Prior. That was her name. I remember asking her why she never went to the toilet. I couldn't understand why my question – couched in genuine admiration for her mighty bladder – should have caused so much offence. I don't think she liked us much. In my memory, she and Brown Owl have merged into one – grey curls, fat calves and a general air of disapproval.

The six-year-old me goes into the house and shuts the door. Mrs Prior looks at me. 'Your mother's not here,' she says. She sounds irritated and anxious all at once.

'Where is she, then?'

'She's gone away for a rest.'

'When's she coming back?'

'I don't know – you'll have to ask your father when he gets home from work.'

'Will she be back tomorrow?'

'I *very* much doubt it.'

'When, then?'

'I've told you, I don't know. I was just rung up and asked to come along to be here when you and Max got home from school. I don't know who it was I spoke to, I'm sure. It wasn't your mother. And it's not as though I haven't got anything else I should be doing today. It's my afternoon for the Nunns at number one. I don't suppose they're best pleased. I'll be off as soon as your father's home. So wash your hands and sit down and have a biscuit and a glass of squash. And then get on with your spellings or numbers or something quiet. Max'll be home from his swimming lesson shortly.'

Mrs Prior was talking rubbish, I was sure of that. I knew my mother hadn't gone away for a rest. Why should she need a rest? She wasn't tired at all. She was always racing around. I knew exactly what had happened.

My mother had told me and Max that lying was a terrible, unforgivable thing. I couldn't remember who had lied to whom or what about, but it must have been something quite major. There were things called white lies, she had told us, which were all right sometimes, but lying – proper lying – was always wrong. Lying destroyed people's lives, she had said, looking as if she was about to cry. It destroyed whole countries. We couldn't quite see how lying could do *that* much damage but we hadn't said anything. It was best not to when she was in that kind of a mood. But some time in the weeks leading up to her disappearance she had lied to my grandmother. I had listened to the phone call, sitting halfway up the stairs in my dark blue brushed-nylon nightie, and I knew, as I heard her tell her mother-in-law that Max and I would not be able to go and stay with her in Oxford after all as we were both ill and weren't up to travelling by train, and then elaborate wildly on the story, that something terrible was happening. We weren't ill at all. It was a complete lie. And not even a white one. If anyone wasn't feeling well, it was *her*, not us. We had tried not to stare at her when she had come home from the dentist some weeks earlier, her face bloated and mottled, her mouth a mess of pulpy red and nothingness where once her teeth had been. She'd had to keep wiping away the blood-flecked spit that trickled from her swollen mouth. She still couldn't speak very well, her 's's were funny. But now she had smart new plastic teeth and, though for some reason she wouldn't speak to our father, wouldn't eat with us and seemed generally angry about everything, she wasn't really any more ill than we were. And we were fine.

After she put the phone down, she had gone into her bedroom, sat down on the floor, and started to cry. I crept on to her lap and put my arms around her but she didn't stop. She didn't even put her arms around me. Max brought her a cup of tea with four sugars in, even though we weren't really allowed to use the kettle, but she left it to get cold. She just sat there crying for hours and hours. We'd seen her cry before, but only once or twice, and nothing like this. We put ourselves to bed and lay shivering in the dark. We heard our father come home, and eventually go upstairs and into the bedroom – and then the screaming started. Some time, in the middle of the night, I woke up. My mother was still crying and shouting at my father. If he was still in the room, he wasn't saying anything.

I got out of bed and went into Max's room. The bed was empty. I opened the cupboard door.

'Listen,' I said. 'Listen to what she's saying.'

But Max slept on, his white blanket pulled up around his ears.

So yes, that day, when I came home to an empty house, I knew exactly what had happened. My mother had lied and then she'd gone mad – that was why she had been so strange when she came to pick me up from Jackie's house – and then she had been put away somewhere. In a way, I was relieved.

'Were you glad?' I asked Max years later in Dorset. We were standing in a field behind the Steiner school at which he had been teaching for the past three years. The fuchsia hedges, barely visible through the freezing fog, were stiff with frost. I had forgotten what English winters could be like, and my whole body rebelled against the biting cold.

'Glad?' he asked.

'When Mum went away. That first time.'

He didn't answer. I turned to look at him. He was gazing over at a group of children bundled up in layers of colourful jumpers, stripy tights, bobble hats and woolly mittens who were playing skipping games, their breath rising in gusts of smoke and merging with the white sky.

*Windmill, windmill going round and round*
*Along came the farmer with grain to grind.*

He was smiling – a smile suffused with such serenity that I wanted to push him to the frozen ground and hit him very hard.

'Is it compulsory to wear hand-knitted rainbow jumpers at a Steiner school?' I asked viciously. 'And Peruvian hats with ear flaps?'

'Sorry?' he replied, not taking his eyes off the children.

'And do you have to be called Griffin or Ocean or... or... Gaia? What if you're called Kevin or Penelope or something? What if your father's a tax accountant or a civil servant, or a bus conductor, and not a bloody biodynamic beekeeper or a llama-breeder or... or a fucking *shaman*? What if you feel uncomfortable cultivating your dreadlocks and your organic dope? If it's not really *you*? What if you want to grow *dahlias*?'

'Why are you so angry?' he asked quietly, turning to look at me.

'Why aren't you?' I shouted, my voice hoarse with cold and fury.

The small skippers stopped their game. They looked over at us, curious to see what would happen next. Max squeezed my arm then walked up to the children. He hugged the smallest one then crouched down and said something to them that I couldn't hear. After a few seconds the children regrouped and two of them began turning the rope.

'Higher!' Max shouted.

The two rope-turners grasped the end of the rope with both hands, their faces screwed up with effort and concentration, and the rope soared high above them.

Max leaped forward and, as the rope touched the ground, he jumped. He did star jumps, tuck jumps; he hopped first on one foot and then the other. His long blond curls danced around his head. The children laughed and yelled out words of encouragement. I watched Max's face. And what I saw was joy. Sheer joy.

'Come on!' he called to me, holding out his arms. But I shook my head and walked away so that the children wouldn't see me cry.

'I didn't know you could skip,' I said later, as we sat by the fire in the little cottage he shared with another teacher and a couple of ancient lurchers he had inherited from a neighbour who had died a couple of years ago. 'You're quite good.' The wood was damp and spat on to the stone hearth. We watched the marooned embers glow and die. The dogs whimpered and kicked in their sleep as they dreamed of rabbits and wide open spaces.

'Thanks.'

'I'm sorry I shouted. Very un-Steiner.'

'It's OK.'

'I just wanted you to tell me that you know what I'm talking about. You were *there*, Max. In your previous incarnation as a quite normal person who didn't wear fingerless gloves and who occasionally brushed his hair.'

Max held out his still-gloved hands in a gesture of conciliation. 'I *do* know what you're talking about,' he said gently.

And I, as usual, felt ashamed. He was always the peacemaker, the good guy, the one who thought the best of everyone, even when all the evidence was there to suggest it would be very much wiser not to. He was the one who would hitch-hike through Europe and end up paying for the driver's petrol. The one who would invite total strangers into his house with no fear of being macheted to death in his sleep. Who could never pass a beggar without giving them whatever he had on him. I remember, when he was about ten, he gave the remains of his Mars bar to a gypsy girl in Dublin. He didn't notice the expression of scorn on her face, and I didn't have the heart to mention it. Max never judged, never criticised. Not like me. Once, when we were walking to school together, and for a reason I can no longer remember, I screamed at him to shut up and drop dead. 'Look around, and say that again,' he said, calmly and a little sadly, nodding up at the top of a garden fence. There, caught in some raspberry netting and hanging lifeless from one spindly foot, was a thrush. It stared at me, its eye opaque and sunken. I kept quiet for a while after that.

During the period that I most adored Max, I'd follow him wherever he went. He never objected when I insisted on accompanying him on his 'Bob-a-Job' missions round the estate. I somehow doubt that the Scout Association still encourages little boys in shorts to go into complete strangers' houses and offer to do anything for them for five pence. It's a shame, in a way. While Max polished the neighbours' silver golfing trophies, weeded their flowerbeds or cleaned their shoes, I would sit drinking Ribena and eating squashed-fly biscuits off brightly coloured melamine plates, chattering about my rabbit or my current favourite book or TV programme to the housewives in their housecoats or floral pinnies.

'And I wanted you to tell me that I'm doing it better. With Susanna,' I said, hoping that his housemate Francesca – who didn't seem able to take her eyes off Max whenever they were together (something Max denied vehemently when I pointed it out to him) – would stay in the kitchen a little longer, perfecting the meal that it was her turn to cook. 'No, I don't mean better. That sounds awful. Unfair. I don't really know what I mean.'

'You're doing fine. Susanna's a lovely child. Extraordinarily lovely, in fact. You know that.'

'And now you're supposed to say, "And you're a great mother."'

'You don't need me to tell you that.'

'But I'd like you to.'

'You're doing absolutely fine. Though of course she'll have inherited most of her finer points from her Uncle Max.'

'Oh, yeah!'

'Or her father.'

'You don't know anything about him.'

'No, but I'd like to. As you know. And you do realise that Susanna is going to want to know, sooner or later?'

'She might not.'

'Oh, Julia,' Max laughed as he walked over to the deep armchair in the corner of the room where Susanna was sleeping. He felt her forehead and stroked her blonde hair off her face. He pulled the blankets up to her chin. Then he came back to the fire and hugged me. His hair smelt of woodsmoke and winter sky. 'You're crazy.'

'Hey,' I said, looking over his shoulder at the mantelpiece. 'A postcard. Where's she gone this time?'

He walked across the room and picked up the card. 'Haven't you had one from here?' he asked, turning it over.

'It probably arrived after I left for England. If it arrived at all. I only seem to get about one in three things through the post.'

'Orvieto.'

'Spain.'

'Italy, actually.'

'I knew that.'

'Of course you did.'

'I *did*.'

'Here, shove up.' Max sat down next to me, then stretched out and lay with his head in my lap, his bare feet dangling over the end of the sofa. 'Tell me a story,' he said, shutting his eyes. He put on his best BBC documentary-maker voice. '*Tell me about your time in Africa.* Ouch! No pinching. Go on. Tell me something.'

And so I described the reddish-brown scrub, the vast baobab trees, the women in their bright batik wrappers and head-dresses harvesting chilli peppers. I told him about the gaggles of little girls in faded cotton dresses and worn flip-flops, who would run into our compound on their way home from school to play with Susanna, picking her up and tying her to their backs or bringing her toys made of plastic bottles or old Coke cans when she grew too big for them to carry around. I told him about the hours I spent in the villages, watching, listening, recording, writing.

'Supper's ready, Max.' Francesca stood in the doorway.

Max rolled off the sofa, stood up and stretched. Francesca gave me a sad half-smile as she led the way to the table.

'This smells great, Frannie,' said Max. 'I'll miss your cooking when I move. You should come too. There's a lot to be said for communal living. Really. Ask my sister. That's what she's studying.'

'Don't,' I warned Francesca, who looked as though she was about to cry as she busied herself serving up a steaming vegetable stew and home-baked bread. 'I can't think of anything worse, myself. But Max swears by it. He thinks it's the way forward and we should all do it.'

A car horn sounds behind me. I look in the mirror and see a woman in a white Volvo estate gesturing towards the house. I am blocking her drive. I start the engine and edge forward a couple of yards. She parks outside the double garage and gets out of the car. She is dressed in her gym kit and is carrying a bottle of water. I watch her as she walks up to the front door and lets herself in. I see her pick up the post from the floor of the glass porch. She pauses for a moment to look at me, then goes inside.

# II

And so there I was in Berlin – 'the cheese head' as he used to call me, when he called me anything at all. And I didn't understand a word anyone was saying. Not one word. I simply couldn't believe it, the first time he hit me.

(SILENCE)

*He hit you?*

No one had ever hit me before. Or even shouted or said anything unkind. I remember that I'd only been in Berlin for about a week. And he pointed to some envelopes that were lying on the hall table and told me to do something with them. I picked them up but I couldn't understand what he was saying. So I asked him to repeat what he'd said – he could understand Dutch perfectly well. But he just walked over to me and hit me on the back of my head. And I dropped the envelopes and he hit me again. 'I forbid you to speak Dutch in my house,' he said. That was the first and last thing he ever said to me in Dutch. And so I had to learn German pretty quickly. You learn everything pretty quickly if the alternative is the back of your father's hand.

*Did your father hit you often?*

And you learn *everything* pretty quickly if all the children at your school jeer when you sit on the boys' side of the classroom because you don't understand what the teacher

29

is saying when she tells you to sit on the girls' side. And if they all make fun of your accent and if they all hate you – the teacher and the pupils and the shopkeepers – because you're from Holland and they hate the Dutch.

*Did your father hit you often?*

He'd summon me into his study. It was always kept locked when he was out. No one was ever allowed in there except by special invitation. He had lovely things in there that he collected on all his business trips. Persian carpets. Swiss clocks. Venetian glass vases. Japanese lacquered boxes. Lovely things. And he'd say something like, 'I saw you today outside school with your hands in your pockets,' and then bang! Or 'I heard you whistling – no girl should ever whistle. You're not a market woman,' and then bang! And boy, could he hit hard! He kept a special comb in his study and it was one of my jobs to make sure all the fringes on his Turkish carpet were combed absolutely straight. And he'd call me in and say, 'Look at this – do you call this straight?' – and then bang!

*How was he with your mother?*

Every morning, he would announce what he wanted for supper and then hand my mother the exact amount of money. He'd literally count it out into the palm of her hand. When he came home from work, he'd go and sit in his study and ring a bell. At which point my mother would carry in his supper tray. I used to dream of putting poison in his wine or ground glass in his sauerkraut. Then he would change and go out for the evening. Berlin was full of cabarets and nightclubs in those days. You'll know that – you've seen the films. You've read those books.

*Isherwood. Yes.*

He must have had a lovely time, don't you think? Occasionally I'd catch sight of him with one of his girlfriends in a restaurant or café on my way home from school at lunchtime. They were always very glamorous, his women, with their bright red lipstick and smart tailored jackets. Well, he was pretty popular wih women. Handsome, clever, well-off, charming...

*Charming?*

Very charming. (SILENCE) We had a furnace in the cellar. And he'd come into my bedroom and look around and say, 'Where did you get that ridiculous toy?' or 'Who gave you that stupid book?' or 'What's that thing you're sewing when you could be doing something useful?' And then I'd have to go down to the cellar with him and he'd open the lid of the furnace and I had to drop the toy, or book, or collection of silk butterflies or whatever else it was, into the flames. And he'd smile as he watched. And if I ever cried, he'd hit me very hard. Here, on the back of my head. Once – it was one of the very few times my grandparents visited from Holland – I remember my grandfather gave me the most beautiful wooden ark. He had made it himself out of old cigar boxes. And in the animals went. Two by two. (SILENCE) I opened my hand like this and in they went. Two by two. And then my father took the ark and he put it on the cellar floor and he made me stamp on it until there was nothing left but a pile of splinters. And in they all went.

(LONG SILENCE)

*And your mother?*

(SILENCE)

Sorry?

*Tell me about her.*

I told you – she was the kindest person there was.

*Did he hit her too?*

31

Sometimes. When the mood took him. When his supper was late, or one of his mistresses had stood him up.

(SILENCE)

*Tell me about her.*

Who?

*Your mother.*

Everyone loved my mother. Except my father, I suppose. Even my father's mistresses liked her. It wasn't just that they felt sorry for her; they really liked her as a person. Once – my God, I haven't thought about this for years. Once, one of them – one of the mistresses – came to our house when my father was at work. I must have been about eleven, I suppose. The woman had a little white dog. One of those fluffy, yappy things. I'd seen her eating with my father in town. They always sat at a window table. She used to put the dog on her lap and feed it bits of meat from her plate. My father must have hated that! I didn't know how my mother would react to this woman coming in to her house – I think she could somehow tolerate all the infidelity and philandering so long as it wasn't shoved right under her nose. They came into the living room and sat down. I was sitting behind one of the armchairs in a corner sewing a badge on to my uniform – so they didn't see that I was in the room. At the time I didn't really understand what they were saying. Something about pregnancy and money. I remember the little white dog came round the back of the armchair and started licking my knees. I had to pinch my nose to stop myself giggling and giving myself away. At first my mother sounded shocked and even angry, and then, as the woman continued to talk, she started laughing. Much later I realised what was going on – the woman was suggesting she pretend to be pregnant to extract the money for an abortion from my father. She was pretty sure he'd do anything to stop his life being inconvenienced in any way. She was offering to share the proceeds with my mother. Fifty-fifty. I don't know if they ever went through with their plan, but I like to think they did.

# Chapter Three

The front door, which was once canary-yellow, is now a dark Oxford blue. The drive has been newly tarmacked. Otherwise everything looks just the same. If I had the courage, I would go up to the door and ring the bell. I would say, 'I used to live here. I was just driving by and remembering things from a long time ago, and I'd very much like to have a look around, if you don't mind.' Do I look like a respectable product of this estate? Like someone who might have a macramé plant-hanger, with spider plants cascading from it, suspended from the roof of my porch? Like someone whose other car could possibly be a Volvo?

Only one window of the house overlooks the drive and the circular green beyond. When we lived here it was my parents' bedroom. Every morning before school, I'd sit on the floor at the edge of the bed while my mother, bleary-eyed and weary from her Mogodon-infused sleep, would haul herself up on to one elbow and brush my waist-length hair. As I look up at the window, I can hear the rasping of the brush, my yelps of irritation as the bristles catch in the dense blonde knots and the hair is corralled into two long plaits. I wear my hair very short nowadays.

Sometimes, in the summer, long after we'd been sent to bed, Max and I would tiptoe in, hide behind the net curtains and peer out enviously at our friends playing on the green. Every so often, a couple of mothers would wander out to call their children in and stand chatting in their cotton slacks or bright summer dresses, a cup of tea or glass of sherry in their hand. We would watch those women with the rapt attention and limited understanding of viewers of a TV documentary about a recently discovered and rather exotic tribe. *Our* mother never went out of the front of the house except to get into her car and, though she was the gardener in the family, she left the pruning of the roses in the front garden to my father.

The curtain is twitching now. The woman is clearly not as practised at surreptitious peering as we were. She is probably noting down the registration number of the car parked outside her house, wondering if she has enough reason to contact Neighbourhood Watch about a middle-aged woman in an elderly Toyota who persists in staring at her house. But there can't be a law against this… whatever it is… this reminiscing with uncertain intent.

Did those mothers ever talk about us, I wonder, as they supervised the picking-up of bicycles, roller-skates, cricket bats and discarded jumpers? Did they ask their children, delicately, if they ever saw our mother, whether she was 'any better now'? Did they ask them if they knew where our mother had been that time she went away so suddenly? Whether her disappearance had had any connection with our regular Sunday outings with our father?

We never said anything to anyone in the Close about those Sundays. We learnt to evade the issue, to change the subject, to lie. Every other week, instead of re-enacting *The Adventures of Robinson Crusoe* on the green or cycling round the estate, or playing doctors and nurses with our friends behind the aptly named Feely family's garden shed, Max and I would be driven through the neat, Sunday-sleepy suburbs, through the litter-blown streets of south London, to an imposing red-brick building on the bank of the Thames. My father would park the car by an elegant Hawksmoor church on whose steps old men in onion-like layers of soiled clothing would gather, surrounded by their bundles and bags, and gaze at us with bloodshot eyes.

The church steps are still home to the poor and dispossessed, with their dirty sleeping bags, their cans of Special Brew and obedient dogs on strings, but they seem younger now, their eyes more blank than bloodshot. The red-brick building is still there, too, with its grand entrance hall, and vast stained glass windows. But now the confident doctors in white coats, the scurrying nurses in their starched white hats and the silent, anxious visitors have been replaced by self-assured young Americans in chinos and trainers, with mouthfuls of chewing gum and expensive metalwork.

'You know the loony bin?' I said to Max, that same winter in Dorset. A couple of days after I'd shouted at the little skippers, I think. 'It's a private American college now.'

'How do you know that?'

'I went there. On my way here.'

'What about Susanna?'

'She came too, of course. I could hardly leave her in the car. She liked the stained glass. And the echoing hall.'

'You're mad!'

'Well, then, it's lucky it's a college now and not a mental hospital, or they might have sectioned me too. Short-circuited *my* brain.'

Max smiled, a little sadly.

'Dad probably thought he was doing the right thing,' he said quietly. 'Sending her there.' It was a Sunday morning, and when I looked at him as he stood by the frozen pond with his icy breath swirling round his head, for a moment he looked eight years old again, engulfed by my father's cigarette smoke, gazing thoughtfully out of the car window as we sped through the empty streets.

'Do you really believe that?'

'I have to. Don't you? If I didn't, it would be unbearable. It would be – ' He stopped.

'Mum never believed it,' I said to him. 'Or forgave him.'

'I know. Did you tell Susanna what the place used to be? Why you'd been there before?'

'No. There didn't seem to be any need to.'

'I thought you were living by some new code of ultimate truthfulness, or something. That there would never be any secrets between the two of you.'

'She's very small.'

'It's her heritage too, in a way.'

'Lucky old Susanna!'

'It wasn't that bad.'

'I'm not saying it was.'

'And I know it's none of my business, but all this secrecy about her father – what's the worst that could happen if she knew a bit about him? If we all did? All I know is that he died very suddenly and that his surname – or first name – may or may not have been Thomas.'

Max hadn't asked any questions three years earlier when he'd found me standing on his doorstep, trembling with misery and lack of sleep, a howling one-year-old in my arms. He just took Susanna from me and jiggled and rocked her until she was quiet then put me into his spare bed. I stayed in that bed for nearly three weeks, curled up in a ball, nursing my grief, while Max brought me meals and looked after his niece and everyone else. By the time I could face seeing anyone or doing anything again, Susanna had learned to walk, using Max's housemates' wheelchairs for support. She cried all the way back to Cameroon.

To reach our mother, we had to climb five flights of steep stone stairs. Unable to resist sidling up to the edge, I would gaze down through the gap in the dark wooden banisters which smelt of beeswax and bare feet, and imagine plunging down, head-first, to land – smashed and bloody – on the intricate Victorian floor tiles. Once, we took a wrong turning off one of the interminable corridors and passed a darkened ward full of people in metal beds, seemingly just sleeping. The patient nearest the door was awake and stared at us as we passed. Max looked back and gave him a polite little wave.

We never saw the room where the electric shock treatments took place.

I don't remember how long my mother spent in that place. I don't know how many times they strapped her down with leather belts, put a block of rubber in her mouth, attached the wires and flicked the switch. I can't remember how often Max and I sat on the bed in her little room, watching her expressionless face, each of us holding one of her hands, trying to tell her things that might make her smile. We became careful storytellers. Or rather, *I* did, and took it upon myself to edit Max's stories as he told them or to nudge or kick him if I could manage to do so without my mother noticing. 'Clara has come to help look after us during the week. It's nice having her to stay,' he'd say to my mother as he fiddled with the rings on the hand he was holding in both of his. 'And it's really nice for Dad to have his mother around.'

My grandmother insisted we call her Clara – she didn't like any of the names our friends called their grandmothers. *Nan? Nanna? Nanny? What sort of stupid names are those? Why would I want to be called after a kind of goat?*

'No, it isn't. It's not at all nice having her to stay,' I'd say. 'She's really bossy. She tells us to lay the table and tidy up and stuff. And make our own beds. It's horrible. And she makes us eat sauerkraut and sausages with disgusting chewy skin and it makes me want to be sick.'

'Dad's taught me to sew on buttons – he's really good at sewing. Ouch! Julia! What did you do that for?'

'Do what? Mum taught me to sew on buttons ages ago, and other stuff, didn't you, Mum?'

I didn't tell my mother that my father had learnt to plait my hair quite expertly, that he did it slowly and gently even if he did incorporate all the knots; that on Saturdays, as Max and I lay on the floor watching *Thunderbirds*, he concocted exotic meals from whatever he could find in the fridge; that once, on a rare occasion when he got home early enough to collect me from school, my teacher, Miss Wharton, had told him that he was 'coping marvellously with everything', and gazed at him with soppy, admiring eyes. 'If there is anything I can ever do to help, all you have to do is ask, Mr Rosenthal. Anything at all.' I didn't tell my mother that it was nice at home without all the shouting and crying.

I didn't tell her these things, but I thought them. Storyteller and traitor.

The weeks and months passed. My grandmother returned home to Oxford, after a pre-Christmas celebration with presents and special German Christmas food that I carefully edited out of the narrative on our next weekend visit.

On Christmas morning, Max bounded into my bedroom. 'Guess what!'

'What?'

'Guess.'

'I dunno. What?'

'We've got the best present ever! Mum's home!'

'She's not. She's in the loony bin. We saw her there last Sunday.'

'No, she's home. She's in her bedroom. I've seen her. Come on!'

But I was filled with such longing and such dread that I couldn't move. Such longing and dread and guilt. I wanted a new bike. Not the mother I'd last seen in her bedroom, sitting slumped on the floor, her back against the wall, screaming at our father. Screaming about her teeth and his silence and the lies, and how he didn't care and what was she being punished for? Screaming that she would rather be dead than live this life. This terrible, lonely, empty life. But when I finally went in, having first quickly ascertained by peeping into the sitting room that it wasn't a case of a new bike *or* my mother, she was sitting up in her bed, smiling at something Max was telling her. My father brought her a cup of coffee. She thanked him in a voice that seemed normal, friendly even. I remember climbing into her bed, putting my arms around her and thinking that things would be all right from now on.

And I suppose that, for a while, they were. One drawer in the kitchen that had previously been home to miscellaneous bits and pieces that didn't belong anywhere else in the house was now full of pill bottles. Our mother called us into the kitchen, opened the drawer, and told us that they weren't sweets, not even the ones that looked just like big red Smarties, and said that we must never touch them. And so we never did, even though I really wanted to bite open the little black and red capsules that reminded me of the guards outside Buckingham Palace, and the thin daffodil-like yellow and green ones, and tip out the tightly packed powder. And I wanted to know how one teeny chalky-white tablet could help you to sleep and how a whole handful could send you to sleep forever.

There is a knock at the car window. I jump and turn my head. It is the woman from the upstairs window. I wonder how she has managed to come out of the house and round the back of the car to the driver's side without me seeing her. I contemplate starting the ignition and driving off but worry that I'll run over her foot if I do that. I roll down the window and smile weakly.

'Hello,' she says. 'It's Julia Rosenthal, isn't it.'

It seems a statement, rather than a question, so I keep quiet.

'You used to live here, didn't you.'

Another statement. I wonder if she is perhaps a lawyer.

'I'm Angie Plaistow. I was at school with you.'

My face must look blank because she continues. 'It's all right. I wouldn't expect you to remember me. I was a few years below you. One of those irritating upper thirds when you were in the fifth form or something. You used to shush me in the library. You're more likely to remember my older sister Becky, from the year above you. You haven't changed a bit.'

She has one of those friendly, open faces. There are smile lines around her pale blue eyes.

'It's so weird. Your name came up about a week or two ago. After all this time. It must be synchronicity or something. I was on the phone to Emily Lancaster who used to live in the house behind this one and was in my class all the way through, and anyway, we were going on about the kids as usual and all that parents and children stuff – Emily's got two girls – and she said she'd read something about your daughter and her uncle in the *Observer* or the *Sunday Times* or something. And she remembered you'd been at the same school as us and used to live in this house. I've been meaning to have a look for it. We get the Sundays most weeks – God knows why – we never seem to get around to reading them. It's probably buried in the paper mountain by my bed.'

My face must look slightly less blank because she pauses for a few seconds and looks at me quizzically.

'Do you want to come in?'

# III

*Tell me about your grandparents.*

My grandparents? God! Was my grandmother a difficult woman! She couldn't have been more different from my mother. What is it you say? Chalk and cheese? She didn't visit us very often but when she did she'd say to me, 'You're just like your father.'

*Why do you think she said that?*

I don't know. She didn't make any attempt to hide how much she disliked my father. Despised him, even. 'The German', she always called him. In the same tone of voice that she used when she talked about 'the Natives' she'd encountered in Indonesia. So I had a pretty good idea what she thought about me.

*Did you mind?*

It would have been nice if she'd liked me. I suppose I wanted her to like me, at least when I was younger – but I didn't really care that much because, when she came, so did my grandfather. And he was such a lovely man. He loved me, I was absolutely sure of that, even if she so obviously didn't. He used to call me his 'little radish' and swing me round by my arms. He smelt wonderful – it was pipe tobacco and gin, I suppose. Far too much of both. But I loved the smell – and he had one of those moustaches that curled upwards like this.

Like a smile. White, with yellow tips from all the nicotine. (SILENCE) And I used to think, I can't be that bad if I have a grandfather like Opa, can I? I can't be the worthless person my father and grandmother think I am, if I'm related to Opa. If he's my grandfather.

(SILENCE)

*There's a tissue there.*

(SILENCE)

*What are you feeling now?*

Nothing. It's all right.

*Do you want to talk about it?*

Not really, no.

(SILENCE)

*Take your time. Here – have another tissue.*

My mother never seemed to bear the slightest grudge at what her parents had done to her.

*What **had** they done to her?*

They left her with the nuns in a convent school in Amsterdam when she was five and sailed to Indonesia with the Dutch army to help suppress the Yellow Peril. And didn't come back once until she was eighteen. I know. It's hard to believe. They left her with the nuns for thirteen years. When my mother told me, I simply didn't believe her. I used to ask her, 'How could they do that? How could they leave you behind?' 'It was complicated,' was all my mother would say. Actually, now I think about it, maybe she minded more than she ever let on. I remember she told me that, each year, her parents would have a huge comb of bananas shipped to the convent. And the one thing my mother never ate was bananas.

*Tell me more about your grandmother.*

More about my grandmother? There's not a lot more to tell. She spoke several Indonesian dialects, with faultless accents apparently. I'm sure her command Indonesian was particularly good. I wouldn't have wanted to be a servant in her household. I suppose I have that to thank her for, if nothing else.

*What to thank her for?*

Her gift for languages. Which I somehow inherited.

*Of course. Sorry. Carry on.*

I know for a fact that she spoke German very well, but during her visits to us, and certainly in the presence of her German son-in-law and her German granddaughter, she claimed not to understand a single word. She must have hated it when her daughter had to marry the first German she met.

*Had to?*

Well, thirteen years in a convent – I don't suppose there was much excitement or sex education there. My mother told me the nuns had taught her French and German, as well as humanities and domestic science, so she was useful to this handsome, charming German engineer who was working so far from home and in need of some female company. I don't suppose he'd counted on quite how much female company he'd get out of it. He hadn't counted on a Dutch Catholic who'd want to keep the brat.

# Chapter Four

'Sorry the place is such a mess,' says Angie as we walk into the house. Normally people say that when their house is looking immaculate but, in this case, it really *is* a mess. I stumble over a lone roller-blade and send the wheels spinning angrily.

'See what I mean? I have been thinking about clearing up. I was coming up with a plan of action while I was on the treadmill, but then I saw you sitting in the car and any excuse to do anything other than tidy. Actually, I've almost given up aspiring to an orderly house. I just about managed to keep the lid on the chaos before number four arrived. But he was the proverbial straw. Geoff doesn't seem to notice the mess, so what's the point, really?'

I smile in agreement, even though I like a tidy house. I think my mother found it quite strange that she'd spawned a daughter who ordered her Puffin paperbacks alphabetically, who lined up her china animals according to species and height and her dolls in national costume by geographical region. She grimaced when once she found me painstakingly combing out the fringes of the sitting room rug with my fingers.

'Aren't you pleased?' I asked her indignantly, my feelings hurt.

'Of course I am,' she replied unconvincingly.

'You don't sound it.'

'No, you've done a lovely job. Thank you.'

'What's wrong with them? They look beautiful when they're not all messed up and tangled.'

'I don't know. It's just one of those things.'

Angie leads me into the sitting room.

'My parents moved here – gosh! – over thirty years ago it must be now. I think it was your parents they bought it from – or maybe the people after them. And then Geoff and I bought it from Mum and Dad when they retired to Eastbourne. It's such a brilliant place for the children to grow up in. So safe. Coffee? Tea? Something stronger?'

'Tea would be great. Thanks.'

'Make yourself at home. I won't be a minute.'

I clear a small space on the sofa and sit down amongst dismembered Barbie limbs and pieces of Lego in the shape of guns and warships.

'Sorry about the un-pc-ness of it all,' Angie calls from the kitchen. 'I tried, really I did. I don't even remember buying the Barbies. They just seemed to appear overnight and then breed. And not a Ken in sight. As for the guns…' She trails off as the kettle begins to bubble noisily. 'Milk? Sugar?'

'Just milk, please.'

'Still, you'll know all about little girls and their dolls.'

I try to remember Susanna's room in Cameroon. White-washed walls; a low metal bed covered with a brightly coloured bedspread. A cave she made for her kittens from cardboard boxes and an old blanket. A pile of books on her bedside table. But no dolls. Was that something else I did wrong?

Angie comes into the room bearing a wooden tray with two mugs and a plate of shortbread biscuits. She hesitates, then nimbly lifts a gym-honed leg and sweeps the contents of the coffee table on to the floor with her foot before placing the tray on it.

'That's better. I should really just put the whole lot in a bin bag and chuck it all out. No one would notice,' she says, good-humouredly. 'You know, the guinea pig had been dead and buried for a fortnight before any of them noticed it was missing. And then Catherine had the nerve to claim to be too upset about its death to go to school! And once she started, Anna and Eleanor felt they had to join in and insisted they couldn't go either. In the end I gave in and the whole lot stayed at home. Mourning away in front of daytime TV. Here, have this mug.'

She passes me the one adorned with dancing princesses.

'I've lost touch with everyone except Emily Lancaster, really. But I went to one of those hideous school reunions a couple of years ago, you know,' she says, cradling her mug in her hands. 'What a mistake *that* was! Everyone seemed to have got fat around the middle, gone grey and married solicitors. So I booked into a gym double quick and got rid of the grey.' She pats her strawberry-blonde hair. 'I thought about making Geoff give up all his lovely conveyancing and uprooting the kids to rural Catalonia but it seemed too much of an effort. You know, the only person from my year who stood out as having done something rather more significant with her life than bed down in the suburbs was Shiranee Batterjee. You must remember her – the only Asian girl in the school in those dark old days. She's a neurosurgeon at Bart's now. Biscuit?'

'No, thanks.'

'Didn't you have a ridiculously beautiful older brother?' she asks.

'I did. Still do, in fact. Max. Still beautiful in a rather middle-aged kind of way.'

'Max! Of course. How could I forget! Becky had the most almighty crush on him for *months*. A violinist, wasn't he?'

'He was, but not any more.'

'Oh, that's a shame. He was very good, I seem to remember.'

'Yes, he was.'

'I'm sure that was why Becky carried on with the violin even though she was absolutely awful at it. Just on the off-chance that, if they ever bolstered up the crummy school orchestra with boys from St Peter's, she might get to sit behind Max. I'm not sure she's shown the same devotion to anyone since.'

'He's always had that kind of effect on girls – and it's never stopped surprising him.'

'So who was the lucky girl who got him in the end?'

'No one did. He's never married. Never even lived with anyone.'

'I'd better not tell Becky that. She might think she'd be in with a chance – not that she's free, of course.'

'Well, when I say he's never lived with anyone, I mean he's had relationships with women – some pretty long-term – but he's never lived with any of them in the conventional couple-living-together way. He likes communities. Groups of unrelated people living together.'

'God! I find living with groups of related people hard enough,' laughs Angie, nodding at the row of framed school photographs and one large wedding portrait on the mantelpiece. 'And what about you?'

'Me?'

'Husband? Children? In case I never do find that article.'

'One child. A daughter. Susanna. Pretty grown-up now. She grew up in Africa – '

'Gosh and there was I thinking Catalonia was exotic.'

'Yes, well – and then in Dorset. At a Steiner school.'

Angie looks puzzled, as though she had once known what a Steiner school was but couldn't quite remember what her opinion had been.

'She studied textiles at Brighton University. It was a toss-up between that or studying music – the flute – at Manchester. And now she lives with her boyfriend in London, not far from me. George. He's a journalist. They seem very happy.'

'Lovely! I just can't imagine getting to that stage – having independent, grown-up children living away from home, earning their own living.'

'Well, I wouldn't go that far. The "earning her own living" bit might take a while. Though she's not been doing badly recently. She's set up a batik business.'

'Emily said something about that – and about her and your brother. But I can't remember the details.'

I can feel myself holding my breath. I exhale as quietly as I can.

'Are you OK?' asks Angie. 'Becky's been suffering with hot flushes too. What we women have to bear!'

'Sorry – yes, I'm fine.'

'And what about your husband?'

'I never had one of those,' I say lightly.

Angie frowns very slightly.

'I live with my partner, Dan,' I add. 'We've been together for about ten years.'

Angie looks relieved, or perhaps I'm just imagining it.

'He's a documentary-maker. I met him when he was going out to make a film in northern Cameroon and wanted some advice. He travels a lot – he's filming in Mumbai at the moment – and I'm mostly based here now. I lecture in anthropology.'

'Sounds lovely.' She smiles. 'Listen, I have to collect Ben – my youngest – from nursery. It's literally just down the road – where the little shopping arcade used to be. I'll probably be about ten minutes by the time I've had a full report on who he's refused to play with today and what food he threw where. Help yourself to more tea and stuff. And there's a new *Hello!* magazine somewhere amongst this mess.'

'Thanks. That's very kind.'

'Mum and Dad built the conservatory on the back but, apart from that, nothing much has changed. We've been meaning to put in a new kitchen for ages but somehow we just never get around to it,' she calls as she goes out of the front door. 'And all that '70s Formica seems to be back in fashion now.'

My mother would like to know that. She had a theory that, if you kept anything long enough, it would come back into fashion. I don't think she ever threw any of her clothes away. She would let them out or down, take them up or in, depending on her size and the prevailing style. And that kept her pretty busy. Where other suburban housewives assuaged their boredom and despair with sherry or chocolate cake or trips to the hairdresser's, my mother bought clothes. Her wardrobes made Imelda Marcos's seem like doll's house furniture. The V&A could have filled a complete floor with her clothes – a history of fashion over the second half of the twentieth century. A history too, I suppose, of her state of mind. A conscientious curator would note the racks and racks of clothes from the 1960s and '70s and rather fewer from the years after that. The collection wouldn't be totally complete. There would be, perhaps, a single glass cabinet for a couple of years during the late '60s. There would be little from the '50s and nothing at all from the decades before that.

I put down the mug, and walk up to the big picture window. There is not much left of the beautiful garden that my mother created out of the building site that surrounded the house when we first moved here. The flowerbeds, with their pink and purple lupins, their sky-blue delphiniums and orange Californian poppies whose pale green conical hats Max and I loved to pull off, have been grassed over. The rockery, whose every piece of stone my mother carried from the car, has been dismantled. The willow tree that she planted is still there, its trunk grown thick and gnarled. The wooden climbing frame with its splintered platform from which we'd jump, or drop parachutes of handkerchiefs and little green plastic soldiers, has been replaced by some kind of aluminium structure with an integral plastic tent in primary colours. The shed we called the Little Wooden House has gone and in its place there is a massive blue trampoline enclosed in a safety net. We kept our mice in that shed, in rows of rusting blue metal cages. Sweet little brown and beige creatures, with shiny fur and beady black eyes. A few weeks after the first batch of mouse-babies were born, and before we mastered the art of mouse-husbandry, they all escaped through the bars. I remember my mother spending a whole afternoon lying on the floor of the shed with a broom, a shoebox and a packet of chocolate buttons, trying to tempt them back into captivity. Max and I helped for a little while, before going off to watch *The Golden Shot* and leaving her to it. 'Bernie the bolt!' We loved it. I think it was *Belle and Sebastian* we were watching that time she carried bucketload after bucketload of damp sand from the drive where it had been unloaded to the sandpit she was building for us at the far end of the garden. She never asked for help and we never offered it. I wish now that we had.

The door to what had been my father's study is shut. My hand hovers over the door handle.

The room is thick with smoke. On his desk are papers, journals, slides, a tumbler of neat whisky. I know those slides well. I like to take them out of their plastic folders when my father is at work and look at them through his little grey and white slide-viewer. There is something faintly pleasurable about the ripples of nausea that spread through me as I gaze at the images of bloody organs and surgical instruments surrounded by green cotton sheets. In some of the pictures, I see my father's gloved hand, spattered with blood, holding a scalpel or a suture, and I feel a rush of pride.

'What now?' he sighs.

'I still can't do this stupid maths.'

I am wearing purple – my colour of choice at thirteen. My haircut is modelled on David Cassidy's. My complexion, sadly, isn't.

'I've just explained it to you,' he says wearily, and rests his smouldering cigarette on a heavy onyx ashtray.

'I know. But can't you just *do* it for me?'

'What would be the point of that?'

'It would be right then, instead of all wrong.'

'But you still wouldn't know how to do it.'

'Who cares? What's the point of maths anyway? It's so boring. You shouldn't smoke,' I say conversationally, as, defeated by my mathematical incompetence and grinding insistence, he picks up a pencil and looks at the exercise book I've slapped down on top of his papers.

'I like smoking.' He fills in the gaps on the squared paper that is rough with my increasingly frantic rubbing out. His abandoned cigarette expires, leaving a snake of cold grey ash.

'We had a film about it at school today. It showed a lung full of tar. And then a whole beaker of horrible black sludge. It was disgusting. Smoking kills, you know.'

'Does it?' my father asks, as he takes out another untipped Player and taps it on the box.

'You should know. You're a doctor.'

'Yes, dear.'

'Why are you smiling? It's not funny.'

'No, dear.' He lights the cigarette with his smooth silver lighter.

'Don't just say *yes dear* and *no dear*. Why don't you listen to me?'

'I am listening.'

'No, you're not. What did I just say?'

'What, dear?'

'You see, you never listen.'

'Yes, dear. Here – I think this is all correct now.'

There is a round bald patch on the top of his head that I've never noticed before. His skin is grey. His hand shakes as he passes me the exercise book and picks up his glass of whisky. He takes a large sip and shuts his eyes, probably hoping that when he opens them I'll have gone away and left him in peace. But I don't want to go away.

'One day you'll just drop dead of smoking and drinking and stuff and I won't have ever even known you.'

'Yes, dear,' he says.

'And if I ever have children, they'll never even know I had a father.'

My father smiles again.

'You should care about all that.'

I can feel my jaw quivering.

'Hello. I'm Ben,' says a small voice. I turn round and there is a child of about four standing just behind me.

'What are you doing standing outside my playroom?' he asks. 'And why are you crying?'

# IV

My mother managed somehow – I don't know how – to save some of her housekeeping money and she'd go with tins of soup and other things to the railway sidings and she'd roll them down the hill to the families with the yellow stars who were living by the railway lines. I used to go with her sometimes. And she was always knitting. She'd knit pullovers and give them to the people who were leaving for Holland and when they got to the border they'd wave them out of the window as a sign and my grandparents would shelter them for a few days before they went on their way.

*Did you wonder why the Jews were leaving?*

Not really. They'd been asked to go, so they were going. I was just glad my mother was making life a bit easier for them. We'd knit together in the evenings when my father was away, but I wasn't nearly as fast as her. We had such a lovely time together then. Or we'd play duets on the piano – my father forbade any music in the house when he was home. I think he thought *owning* a piano was one thing – the sign of a cultured household – but anyone playing it – or, worse still, enjoying playing it – was quite another thing. Or I'd practise my English. That was the one thing at school that I was *really* good at. And it felt so wonderful – to really excel at something. To be better than all of my classmates who had teased me so much when I arrived at the school and sat at the back of the classroom, not understanding a word anyone was saying. Who had hated the little Dutch newcomer so much. In the end I was better than all of them. At German *and* English. Better at English than most of the teachers. I had this textbook with a photograph of Trafalgar Square on the cover – with those huge black lions and the fountains and Nelson's Column – and that was the one place in the world I was desperate to visit. I don't know why. There was just something so special about it. I wish I still had that book.

*Do you have anything from that time?*

Nothing. No, not nothing. A small red leather notebook. Like a diary. And a tiny wooden angel.

*A wooden angel?*

Once, my father announced that he'd been called to Cologne on urgent business, so my mother took me to the Christmas Market. All those stalls selling the most beautiful things. Tiny wooden figures and gingerbread stars and spicy sausage. That must have been the first and probably only time my mother met my best friend Helga Lessing. Bringing friends home was not something my father allowed. Helga was there with her parents and her two brothers. Her father was a butcher who'd been unemployed for a long time but their luck had turned. They'd just moved into a house in the centre of Berlin that had suddenly become empty for some reason. We know why now, of course. Hindsight! That wonderful thing! Before that, they'd all slept in one room somewhere – I don't know where – I never went. And I remember Herr Lessing said something to my mother like, 'You must be so pleased with your daughter – all those athletics medals she's been winning. She's precisely the kind of girl our Führer would be proud of, don't you think?' And my mother just looked at the swastikas on their lapels and didn't say anything. My mother – who was always so polite and kind to everyone. And I remember Herr Lessing looked rather put out as they walked over to the carousel. I was furious with my mother. I couldn't believe that she could dismiss them like that just because they were so much poorer than us. Because Helga's father was a butcher and not an engineer. But she said, 'How much money they do or don't have has nothing to do with anything.' And she took me by the hand and led me over to the stall that sold little carved figures. 'I'm going to buy you an angel,' she said. 'An angel for my angel. You choose the one you like best.' They were so beautiful, those tiny wooden angels. Some were playing trumpets; some were holding books; some were plucking at harps or singing. There was one which was gazing upwards, its mouth a little red O. And it looked to me as though its heart was bursting with the joy of singing. It was so small that if you put it in the palm of your hand and closed your fingers, no one would ever know it was there. And I thought that this lovely tiny thing would surely be able to escape the furnace. Just after we got home, a telegram arrived, addressed to my father. And my mother opened it very carefully and it said something like '*Unable to meet you in Cologne as planned, so sorry. With love from your own Katharina.*' And my mother said – and I could see that she was half-smiling, even though she looked worried – 'Your father's urgent business meeting has been very unexpectedly cancelled. You'd better hide the wooden angel very carefully and go to bed quickly. He'll be home any minute and I can promise you he won't be in a good mood.' And sure enough, about half an hour later we heard the front door slam. And the next day there was a bruise on my mother's face. She had tried to cover it up with powder, but I knew it was there.

# Chapter Five

'Hello, I'm Julia,' I say to the small boy called Ben. 'And I've got something in my contact lens. It's making my eyes water.'

'They're doing sunflowers,' Angie says as she comes into the sitting room carrying a bright blue Thomas the Tank Engine lunchbox and holding out a small navy blue sweatshirt daubed with orange and yellow paint. 'Are you all right?'

'She's got something in her toncat lens,' says Ben with authority.

'Oh, that can be so painful! Why don't you use the mirror in the downstairs loo?'

'Thanks.'

'I'm going to have another cup of tea. Would you like one?'

'Yes, thanks. Sorry about this. I won't be long.'

'No hurry.'

'Can I see your toncat lens?' asks Ben.

'No, you come with me, Ben. I'll get you some juice and a biscuit.'

'But I want to see the lady's toncat lens.'

'She won't be able to sort it out with you peering at her. Now come on. I've got Jaffa Cakes.'

I sit on the loo seat, and bury my head in my lap. I haven't cried about my father since the day my adolescent prophecy was fulfilled and now I can't seem to stop.

'What's the matter now?' my father would have sighed, as he lit another cigarette or poured himself another cut-glass tumbler of neat whisky. Or 'It'll be better in the morning,' if the trouble was more medical than metaphysical. He said that to Max, just minutes before Max's eardrum perforated. And to me the time I trod on a nail on the drive which went through my shoe and embedded itself in my foot. 'Good thing I didn't drive over that nail,' he said. 'It would have punctured the tyre.'

After what feels like quite a long time, I get up and look in the mirror. My mascara has run and the whites of my eyes are bright pink. I look more than a little mad. I splash cold water on my face and rub at the black smudges with loo paper. I practise polite smiles. When I return to the sitting room, Ben is sitting cross-legged on the carpet in front of the television, eating biscuits and watching a train pulling into a railway siding. 'I'm sure they've got a mild form of Asperger's, don't you think?' Angie asks pleasantly as she puts down her copy of *Good Housekeeping* and pours the tea into mugs.

'Sorry?'

'Train enthusiasts. When Geoff and I moved in together, I found all these old notebooks of his, full of numbers and cryptic references to things like Crewe Works and Clapham Junction. And Didcot. It made me feel all funny – as though I'd come across a secret stash of well-thumbed porn mags or something.' She nibbles at a biscuit. 'Geoff insists it's no odder than birdwatching, but I'm not convinced. I'm afraid the trainspotting gene seems to have passed down through the father's line, as you can see. To the male of the species, at least. How's the contact lens?'

'Much better, thanks.'

'They can be a real bugger, can't they? I once spent a couple of hours looking for a missing lens that was sitting on my cheek the whole time. And God knows how often I've had to get Geoff to unscrew the U-bend.

'I wonder if there's anyone in the Close you'd still remember,' Angie muses as she nurses her mug of tea and looks lovingly at the hunched, absorbed figure of her son. 'I'm pretty sure there isn't. The Croziers were the last of that era to go, I think. They retired to Spain, I seem to remember my parents said. And then one of them – her, I think – got one of those horrible cancers – pancreatic or something – and died very quickly. There's a lovely family who moved down from Birmingham next door now. He's something in the drinks business and she's a life coach. They've got a son about Ben's age but rather better behaved. And twins on the way. IVF. Were you hoping to see anyone else on the estate?'

'No. I hadn't planned to. I hadn't planned to come here, actually.'

Angie looks a little mystified. I feel I owe her some kind of explanation in return for the mugs of tea and equanimity.

'I've got an appointment with a solicitor not far from here at four-thirty and I got all my timings completely wrong. I had one of those mornings...'

'Tell me about them!'

'And I suddenly thought that I'd come and see what Eynsford Park Estate looked like, thirty years on.'

'And what does it look like?'

'Different. But still very familiar. It's weird.'

'This is the first time you've ever been back?'

'It is. I've lived abroad a lot. And what about you?' I ask, hoping Angie won't notice the subject changing direction. 'What did you do after school?'

'French at Goldsmith's, then a PGCE. I never did the probationary year, though. The teaching practice just about finished me off. They don't tell you on the course what to do when thirty-five twelve-year-olds fart at a pre-arranged time, or when a child comes to school every day with just a Crunchie bar in his lunchbox, or what to say when a social worker comes in to investigate an alleged case of incest. You know, in one of my classes, there were only two children who were living with both their biological parents. When I was at the High School – it was probably the same for you – there wasn't a single girl in my class from a broken home. I suddenly realised what a cushy job all our teachers had. The worst thing I ever did was hand in my RE homework a day late. And that was only the once.'

'I bit Jennifer Black.'

'Sorry?'

'I bit Jennifer Black. I ran at her from the far end of the playground and bit her in the chest.'

For a while neither of us says anything. Angie Plaistow develops a keen interest in shunting locomotives. I don't know where that memory was unearthed from, but I can see Jennifer very clearly – with her irritating frizzy blonde hair and horrid little upturned nose. I had regretted the incident immediately. Not because of the damage I'd inflicted – I was rather proud of the mouth-shaped mark that Jennifer tearfully demonstrated to an eager, somewhat shocked, crowd of seven-year-olds – but because I was worried that Mrs Black would come round to our house and shout at my mother. For days I dreaded the phone or doorbell ringing and, whenever it did, I would hold my breath as I hovered behind my mother, only letting it go when I was sure it wasn't Mrs Black. She never did speak to my mother as far as I know, but Jennifer announced rather proudly, the day after the incident, that she wasn't allowed to talk to me ever again. Ever.

'I've got to pick up the rest of the brood in a bit,' says Angie, looking at her watch. 'And I promised I'd collect Geoff's dry-cleaning.'

'Yes, I must get going too. Thanks so much for the tea.'

'It was lovely seeing you. Come on, Ben, shoes on. What time did you say your appointment was?'

'Four-thirty.'

'You'll still be terribly early.'

'It's fine. Really.'

'Look, you're welcome to stay here.'

'That's very kind, but – '

'Honestly. I won't be long and I'm sure you don't want to sit in the car outside the solicitor's for hours.'

If I stay, I could look around the house. I don't know if the feeling I have at the pit of my stomach is dread or exhilaration.

'I'm sure you don't want a complete stranger sitting here eating your biscuits while you're out.'

'You haven't touched any of my biscuits – and anyway, you're not exactly a complete stranger. You could have a look around the house if you like. See what's changed. Honestly, it's no problem at all. I'd say if it was.'

'Well, thanks. I'd like to do that – if you're really sure you don't mind.'

'Just be careful as you go into the end bedroom. Catherine has a slightly disturbing fascination for all things military and the room could well be booby-trapped. And I'd love to hear more about you and your daughter. Emily said I'd find the article really interesting.'

'No, look, I'll go. You'll have loads of things to do once you've picked everyone up.'

'Don't be daft. It's fine. Really. Just make yourself at home. Come on, Ben, I said shoes on.'

I finish my tea as Angie and Ben get ready to go out, and wait until I hear the front door close behind them before going upstairs.

I stop on the small landing halfway up the stairs and sit down on the top step. Max and I used to crouch here after we'd been sent upstairs to bed, quiet as spies, as we tried to make out what was going on in that strange downstairs night-time world from which we were excluded. There wasn't very much to hear, but that didn't deter us. My mother spent most evenings alone, waiting for my father to come home from the hospital, sewing or watching television or playing slow, sad pieces on the piano. When they were both home, we might hear footsteps on the parquet floor, the creak of the drinks cabinet door, an indistinct question from my mother, a pause, the equally muffled answer from my father, the footsteps receding, the study door shutting, the TV going on. Cilla. Anyone who had a heart.

Sometimes, I would wake up in the night to the sound of my parents arguing and come and lie here, curled up in a little ball, my nightie pulled taut over my feet, envying Max as, safe in his cupboard, he slept through my mother's shouting and my father's silent response.

'They all treat me the same. Like I'm the enemy. Your mother, the whole lot of them,' I once heard her cry out, her voice hoarse with despair. 'Well, don't they? Why don't you ever support me? Why aren't you ever on my side?'

'What, dear?'

*What, dear.* I don't think I ever once heard my father use my mother's name. It was as though she didn't have a name. The few friends of mine or Max's who met her called her Mrs Rosenthal, my grandmother called her *your mother* and we called her Mum – and that was that.

On Thursday afternoons, we were banished to this landing with a packet of Bourbon biscuits. We used to sit on the top step, nibbling away at the dense chocolate filling as we listened to Schumann's *Kinderszenen* or the *Moonlight Sonata*, interspersed with the piano teacher's sporadic words of encouragement. After an hour or so, my mother would open the frosted glass door and we'd be called downstairs for our own lessons. I hated the piano but loved the piano teacher. Mr Elliot was an old man – he told me he was fifty-four – and reminded me of the doctor in *Brief Encounter* – a film that Max and I had yawned our way through one rainy afternoon some time before the advent of our own matinee idol.

For the love of Mr Elliot, with his dark brown slicked-back hair and his hazel eyes that disappeared into a mass of crinkles when he smiled, I struggled hopelessly with bass clefs, treble clefs, minims and quavers. I did everything I could to make sure he would never realise that I couldn't make any sense whatsoever of the symbols on the sheets of music that he placed in front of me unless I'd first heard the piece played through a few times.

'All right, Julia. What about a new piece? This one looks a lot of fun. "In Grandmother's Garden". Just two notes for the left hand to worry about and the right hand's playing the tune. It's in four four and don't forget the F sharp here and here. Right. Off you go.'

'Mr Elliot?'

'Yes, Julia?'

'How many times have you seen *The Sound of Music*?'

'Just the once. What about you?'

'Three times. Sarah Woodley in my class has seen it seven times.'

'Good gracious. All those singing nuns and stormtroopers. Now, let's start with the left hand.'

'I'd quite like to be a nun.'

'Would you?'

'I'd like to give all my things to the poor and wear a wimpole.'

'I'm not sure many nuns wear wimples these days but I'm sure you'd look very fetching in one. Now, Julia – the left hand starts on a G. This G.'

'Mr Elliot?'

'Yes, Julia?'

'What's your favourite kind of torture?'

'Torture?'

'Yes. You know – like being rolled down a hill in a barrel full of nails or having a tap dripping on to your head for years and years, or one of those racks where they turn the handles until your arms and legs come right out of their sockets and fall on to the floor.'

'I think I'd go for the barrel full of nails. I tell you what, why don't I play this through for you a couple of times before you start? You count me in.'

Max – who also loved Mr Elliot, though perhaps not quite as passionately – took it all very seriously and learned very quickly, before transferring his allegiance to the violin, if not the violin teacher.

When Mr Elliot was in the house, everything felt different. The house took on a festive, party atmosphere. My mother laughed. We all laughed. Quite often he would stay for tea.

'Come again tomorrow!' Max and I would beg as he threw his leather music case into the back of his grey Austin. 'Go on! You wouldn't mind, would you, Mum?'

And so, by the spring of 1967, Mr Elliot – Roland as he asked us to call him – was coming to see us most days. On sunny afternoons after school, my mother would drive us all into the country where Max and I climbed trees and looked for beetles while she and Roland sat on a tartan rug on the grass watching us. Sometimes we'd feel rather sorry for our father, who was stuck at work saving the lives of small children and missing out on all the fun. One day during the summer holiday he came home, after what must have been an unusually quiet day at the hospital, to find the four of us flushed with sunshine and happiness, eating Battenberg cake in the garden. He looked slightly surprised to see us all, I thought.

'Roland.'

Roland stood up to shake my father's hand. 'Oscar. Good to see you again. How are you?'

'Fine, thank you, and you?'

'Fine. Enjoying the lovely weather and the delightful company.'

'Are you?'

My father looked around as though wondering which particular delightful company Roland was referring to. Then he glanced in the direction of his study.

'Well, I must get – '

'Why don't you take a day off work and come out with us tomorrow, Dad?' I asked. 'Roland's coming if he can cancel one of his lessons and we're going to Rochester Castle.'

I can't remember what he replied, but I do remember that he never took up the offer of accompanying us on what Max and I increasingly came to think of as our family outings. My mother was very happy during those months and so Max and I grew happier and less wary, less scared she might suddenly go mad again and disappear once more. Her piano lessons got longer and longer, though, oddly, we never heard much Schumann or Beethoven, or anything else really. She sometimes forgot to give us biscuits. My father would come home late in the evening to find Roland and my mother watching *The Forsyte Saga* together. He didn't have a TV of his own.

That was the year we went on holiday to Spain – me, Max, Mum and Roland. The idea was that we would drive down to a villa belonging to a friend of Roland's, camping on the way, and my father, who was far too busy at work to take more than a week of leave, would fly out to join us once we had arrived.

Things didn't go completely to plan. The car journey was strangely tense. For a reason neither Max nor I could understand, our mother refused to share her compartment of the tent with Roland and chose, instead, to sleep in the car. Edgy with incomprehension, Max and I lay in our section of the tent during those warm Mediterranean nights, giggling as we listened to Roland snoring away on the other side of the canvas dividing-wall or spied on him in his voluminous underpants and string vest. Once we caught sight of his dangly willy and had to burrow deep into our sleeping bags to muffle our hysterical laughter.

The night before we arrived at our Spanish villa, I woke to the sound of voices outside the tent. I nudged Max awake and we shuffled, caterpillar-like in our sleeping bags, towards the entrance. We unzipped the door a couple of inches. My mother and Roland were sitting on the ground a few yards away. Roland was holding her hand.

'Of course I can't,' we heard her say, her voice husky with misery or anger, we didn't know which.

'Why not?'

'Why do you think?'

'I don't know. That's why I'm asking you.'

'Because I can't. And I can't go on like this. It's killing me.'

If Max hadn't sneezed at that point, we might have found out what it was she couldn't go on doing. What was killing her. But he did and we didn't. For a while we thought she was just upset because she'd got sick of sleeping in the car, but, when we got to the resort near Malaga, and Roland stayed at the villa and the rest of us moved into an apartment on the beach to await our father, we began to think it might have been something else. It was only the three of us on the long, hot drive back to England.

Shortly after we got home, we heard the familiar sound of Roland's Austin outside the house. Max and I rushed down the corridor to open the door, ready to hurl ourselves into his arms as we always did.

'Just go upstairs,' my mother said, blocking our route to the door. 'We're out.' We stood behind her listening to the incessant ringing of the bell.

'But he knows we're here. He heard us,' I whispered, feeling both desperately sorry for Roland and terribly ashamed at being party to this deception. 'He'll think it's really rude. Let him in! Please, Mum.'

'Go upstairs.'

'He wants to see us. He's come over specially.' By now I was no longer whispering.

'It's not you he's come to see.'

'Open the door. Please, Mum,' Max begged, the corners of his mouth quivering.

'Go upstairs!'

So Max and I stood at her bedroom window, and watched through a crack in the net curtains as Roland Elliot drove out of the Close and out of our lives. We never heard our mother play the piano again.

# V

My father used to sit in his summer house at the end of the garden and listen to the foreign broadcasts on the wireless even though it was absolutely forbidden. Or probably because it was forbidden. He *hated* Hitler – thought he was a ridiculous little failed painter – said we'd lose this stupid war. For a long time, we were the only people I knew without a swastika in the house, and when we finally got a flag he insisted on buying the smallest one he could find. It was about *this* big. I always hoped that the SS man who lived at the end of our road would hear him listening to the wireless and come and get him taken away. My God! I'd have been so happy if that had happened. I came so close reporting my father – I got as far as dialling once – then put the phone down. I don't know why I didn't do it. I wish I had.

*I'm surprised.*

That I didn't report him?

*No. About your father and Hitler. I'd have thought your father would have had Nazi leanings. That he would have been a Party member.*

Are you supposed to have opinions?

*We agreed there weren't any rules. But sorry, carry on.*

No – you go on. Tell me what else you're surprised about. I'd like to know. It'd make a nice change.

*No, go on. Please.*

My father didn't care about Hitler's policies. Or what was going on in Europe. My father didn't like Hitler because he didn't like anyone telling him what to do or how to live. Not for any other reason.

*I see.*

He was furious when he got a letter from some official or other saying he shouldn't be buying things from Mr Finkelman's hardware shop. He'd be damned if he'd let those Nazis tell him what he could and couldn't do. If he wanted to buy a lawnmower from Mr Finkelman, he damn well would, and an English one at that. He was a great admirer of British engineering. Why are you smiling?

*Sorry. Carry on.*

He never let me go anywhere with my friends, or do anything nice, but then, when I joined the Bund Deutscher Mädel, suddenly he couldn't stop me. You know what that is, I assume?

*Like the girls' Hitler Youth?*

Something like that. I'd say, 'Father, there is this camp I have to go to,' or 'that meeting I have to attend,' or 'that bomb site I have to help clear,' and there was nothing he could do about it. I remember the most wonderful spring day, the sun was shining through the birch trees and the leaves were that lovely pale green, and we marched through the woods in our uniforms, Helga and me up front, leading the troupe, singing incredibly loudly. And the song was about spring, and trees, and God knows what else, and I didn't think I'd ever felt so happy.

(LONG SILENCE)

'But four young Oysters hurried up
  All eager for the treat;
  Their coats were brushed, their faces washed,
  Their shoes were clean and neat.'

I was sitting in the garden learning that poem for an English exam the day war was declared. It's quite funny, don't you think?

*Funny?*

Don't you know the poem?

*I'm afraid I don't.*

So much for an expensive education.

*Indeed.*

Well it doesn't end well for the oysters.

'"A loaf of bread," the Walrus said,
  "Is what we chiefly need:
  Pepper and vinegar besides
  Are very good indeed – "'

*Oh. I see.*

My father was furious when he heard the news. He rushed out of the summer house shouting, 'I said he's an idiot – your great friend the warmonger Adolf Hitler. What a fool! We'll lose the war. You wait and see!' It was as though it was all *my* fault – the war and the fact that he'd now have the terrific inconvenience of not being able to get to Italy to buy his handmade suits and shoes. My fault that the supply of imported Atco lawnmowers would be interrupted.

*And how did you feel? When war was declared?*

I can't remember. It sounds stupid, but I really can't remember.

*And England being the enemy?*

What about it?

*What did you feel about England being the enemy? When you'd been so keen to go there. To learn English.*

I didn't think England was the enemy. I didn't think like that at all. I don't know what I thought. You want me to say something profound and meaningful about the war. About sides. There's nothing like that to say.

# Chapter Six

'CATHERINE'S BEDROOM – KEEP OUT!!' it says on the door in blood-red ink on yellow paper. And underneath it in slightly smaller print, 'I MEAN IT OR YOUR DEAD.'

I open the door of my old bedroom very cautiously; nothing falls on my head. The plain white textured wallpaper has been replaced by repeating pink and white ballerinas gamely pirouetting between the posters of scowling marines in camouflage combat gear and helmets sprouting abundant autumn foliage. The pale oak bookshelves that my mother built for me are still there, now painted matt cherry-red. In place of my rows of alphabetised Puffin books and my china animals are a glossy brochure advertising careers in the army, a pile of magazines featuring pouting teenage girls in skimpy vests and too much make-up, a copy of *David Copperfield* that looks like a school set text, a small TV and a laptop computer. I somehow doubt that Catherine's summer evenings are spent sitting on the windowsill reading until it is too dark to see the words on the page.

I don't remember ever being read to as a child. Reading was what I did to other people, whether they liked it or not. From the moment that Jennifer Black was undeservedly promoted to a higher level of *Janet and John* than me – something I felt was so monstrously unfair that I wept from the moment I got home until my mother went out and bought the book for me and then sat and listened to me reading it all the way through – I vowed to be the best reader in the school. My mother would sit on my bedroom floor, leaning against the bed, her eyes shut, while I read her my favourite books over and over again. She seemed to enjoy the experience. The only book she eventually begged to be spared was *Brer Rabbit*. She claimed not to understand what it was all those Brer Foxes, Brer Bears and Brer everyone elses were talking about. Perhaps it was my Southern States accent that let me down. I don't think that my favourite Noel Streatfeild books did much for her either, with their eccentric English guardians and shabby-genteel houses on the Cromwell Road inhabited by unfeasibly gifted dancers, skaters and violinists in sensible macs and sturdy shoes; but those she tolerated in silence.

'You know, Mum, you never read,' I once observed, my rendition of *Great Expectations* finished for the evening. I was leaning over the edge of my bed, brushing her hair and teasing it into ever more outlandish styles.

'That's because you like reading to me.'

'No, I mean I've never seen you read a book, ever.'

My mother didn't say anything. I carried on with my hairdressing for a while.

'Are you sure you can read?' I asked eventually.

She jerked her head away from my hands. 'Of course I can read! I used to be just like you – reading all the time. I had even more books than you've got. And then. Well, that's another story.'

'And then what?'

'And then,' she said, struggling to her feet, 'one day a bomb fell on my bedroom and they all got burned.'

'Was that in the Blitz?'

We had touched, very briefly, on the Second World War when we were presented with a middle-aged supply teacher from the north for History – the first male teacher ever to gain access to the staff room of my all-girls school. He had come to fill in for Miss Harvey – one of the teachers we knew to have tragically lost her fiancé in that very war. Caroline

Statham said, wasn't it a bit of a coincidence that Miss Harvey had been off school ever since her friend Miss Kingston, who taught sixth form science and who had also reputedly lost her fiancé in the war, had moved away to be deputy head of a girls' school in Norwich? I said I didn't think so really, and Caroline had rolled her eyes and carried on carving Max's name into her desk with her compass.

Mr Fielding's grasp of the Tudors had turned out to be rather slight, so, having taught us a rhyme to help us remember the order and upshot of Henry VIII's six marriages, he had decided to teach us about something 'a little more recent and a great deal more bloody relevant'. Unfortunately, I could remember a lot more about his swearing in class, his badly fitting jacket and his unfamiliar vowel sounds than what D-Day and the Normandy landings were all about.

'Mum?'

'What, Julia?'

'I said, was it in the Blitz that you lost all your books?'

'Something like that. Now, goodnight.' She leant down and kissed me on the forehead. 'Sleep tight, and don't turn your light on again the moment I've gone out of the room. And don't sit reading on the windowsill, either.'

And that was the end of that discussion.

I walk over to the window. The bedroom overlooks the thinner L of the garden. There used to be a little pond here in which Max's goldfish was reputed to live. Max had won it at a local fair and named it Looby Loo. As if in response to the ignominy of being named after Andy Pandy's absurdly ineffectual sidekick, on release it had drifted passively out of its plastic bag and disappeared into the murky depths, not to be seen again. We would often sit by the pond, Max and I, poking holes in the emerald surface so viscous with pondweed and algae that the sticks could practically stand up on their own. Once, on a particularly warm evening, the fish – now about four times its original size – had risen slowly to the surface like an ancient submarine, its bright orange fins leisurely parting the lush vegetation.

'Oh, my God!' Max stared first at the massive fish and then past me, his eyes wide with terror.

'What?' I panicked.

'There's an evil dwarf behind you.'

I spun round, letting out a piercing squeal, and Max collapsed on the lawn. He only stopped laughing when I knelt on his chest and squeezed him very tightly around the neck.

'All right! All right! It was just a joke,' he gasped, struggling out of my grasp. 'You shouldn't watch *The Singing Ringing Tree* if it scares you so much.' But each Thursday afternoon I would be drawn to the sofa to watch, appalled, as the terrifying events of the strange Eastern European fairytale unfolded in our sitting room.

Throughout my life I have had a recurring dream. Out of a lightly swirling mist a lake rises and takes shape. The banks drip with ferns and lichen. From behind a rock, a dwarf peers, its goatlike eyes bulbous and unblinking. A pulse throbs angrily in its squat, thick-set neck. Its menacing fingers grip the wet stone, squeeze the dense, dark moss. The dwarf sidles round the rock, a square head framed with wild, wiry hair followed by a long, powerful torso, on short, bowed legs. Still peering round, he waddles, scuttles, crab-like, stopping and starting, stopping and listening, down to the lake, and crouches, elbows splayed, at the water's edge. A watery sun breaks through the thin grey cloud, catches the ripples as a great golden fish rises majestically through the water, bubbles rising and breaking, shattering the dwarf's reflection into a hundred ripples. A branch cracks; the fish glides back down into the black water; the dwarf freezes, taut, alert, sniffs the damp air. Then is gone.

Max was right. I shouldn't have watched it.

Perhaps rather rashly, given Angie's warning about booby traps, I slide the cupboard door open. Catherine's cupboards are full, but not as full as mine used to be. My shelves used to be stuffed to bursting. Unlike most of my friends, whose mothers would go through their belongings periodically, consigning broken or outgrown toys to the Scouts' jumble sales, my mother let us keep absolutely everything. Somewhere, in a set of plywood packing cases – now in Max's attic, I think – we still have every single childhood book, toy, board game and school exercise book that we have ever owned.

No dolls, though. I never went through a doll phase. I didn't need to – I had the real thing. For several years – probably from the ages of about nine to twelve, and before I reached the stage where I would have gladly chosen death over being seen out in public with my father – I would often accompany him on his regular weekend calls to one of the hospitals at which he worked. Almost every Sunday afternoon the phone would ring and my father, after a brief, hushed consultation, would announce to us that he had to go to work and would be back in a couple of hours. I could never understand why this made my mother so tight-lipped and angry. Surely doctors couldn't help having to go to work at the weekend? Leaving Max to his violin practice and my mother to the debris of Sunday lunch, we would head off in the car away from Tenterden Close and my mother's brooding discontent.

I loved the comfortable, nicotine-imbued silence of those car journeys, during which my father would smoke cigarette after cigarette, flicking first the thin plastic film, then the silver paper, then the burning stubs and finally the empty cigarette packet out of the car window. I rather admired the way he could steer with his knees, even while driving round roundabouts, as he extracted his lighter from deep within his trouser pocket. There was slightly less flashing and hooting from swerving cars once he upgraded his car to one with a built-in cigarette lighter. Sometimes he would listen to classical music or the news on the radio, but mostly he just stared ahead, thinking.

'What are you thinking about, Dad?' I asked once, having studied his impassive profile for several miles of London suburb.

'What, dear?'

'What do you think about all the time when you drive to work or sit at your desk in the evenings?'

'I don't know.'

'You must know. You're the one thinking.'

'Yes, dear.'

'So what is it you think about? Work?'

He didn't reply, hoping, no doubt, that I would get bored with interrogating him so we could revert to our companionable hush.

'Go on – what do you think about? Me?' I asked, hopefully.

He smiled. 'Yes, you. All the time. Every minute of the day and night.'

'Why do you never take anything I say seriously?'

'I do, dear.'

At the hospital, I'd be delivered to Curtis Ward on the third floor where Sister Collins, her hands tucked into the bib of her apron, would take me on a personal ward-round, briskly pointing out the babies who were well enough to be taken out, changed, bathed and played with. It seems unthinkable now, that a ten-year-old child would be let loose in a ward full of babies, particularly seriously ill ones, but, as far as I remember, I never dropped or drowned one.

After an hour or two on the ward, I would wander into the Sister's office and there would be my father, smoking and drinking coffee and looking much happier and more relaxed than he ever did at home. In Sister Collins' office, my father became chatty – jovial, even. He seemed to occupy more space. I didn't particularly like Sister Collins with her air of cool efficiency, her sardonic smile, and the annoying way she looked at my father as though he was the cleverest and most fascinating person she had ever met. But my father seemed to like her a lot. It couldn't have been her looks, unless it was the pale blue uniform he liked. It wasn't that she was really ugly or anything like that, but she wasn't nearly as pretty as some of the other younger nurses who would glance at me as they got on with their tasks. And, with her frizzy brown hair and hint of a moustache, she was not nearly as attractive as my mother. Below the ruffled cuffs of her short sleeves, her arms were pale and blotchy and, though I can no longer remember them, I'm sure her calves would have been on a par with those of Brown Owl and Mrs Prior.

It must have been the admiration my father liked – he certainly didn't get much of that at home. My mother could go for days without speaking to him. I wasn't sure that he noticed or, if he did, that he really minded. I think he preferred the stony silence to her miserable rants, to which he'd inevitably respond, 'What, dear?' before disappearing into his study via the drinks cabinet.

My interest in babies faded as my interest in boys increased, and my weekend trips to the hospital became rarer and rarer and finally stopped altogether. I'd almost forgotten about Sister Collins when one day, when I was about fifteen, my father did something very strange.

'I've invited someone for dinner,' he announced in the kitchen shortly after my mother had gone off on the first of her Open University residential weekends.

I put down the sheet of quotations from *Coriolanus* that I was learning for my end-of-term English exam and stared at my father. In our house, no one ever came for dinner. No one ever came, full stop. 'Sorry?'

'I've invited someone for dinner.'

'Who?'

'Sister Collins.'

I was suddenly filled with a feeling of dread so powerful

that I could barely breathe.

'Why are you doing that?'

'What, dear?'

'Why's she coming here?'

'To discuss a chapter of a book I'm writing,' he replied, unconvincingly, opening the kitchen cupboards and rummaging through the tins of condensed tomato soup, pots of liver pâté and jars of gherkins. 'Tell Max, could you…?'

'Who?' asked Max, lowering his violin from his chin and letting the bow hang by his side.

'Sister Collins.'

'Who's she?'

'That nurse in charge of the ward where I used to go to play with the babies.'

'Oh, yeah? What's he cooking?'

'What do you mean, what's he cooking! She can't come here.'

'Why not?'

'She just can't.'

'What's so bad about her?'

'Nothing.'

'So why are you getting your knickers in a twist? Dad's a great cook.'

'That's not the point!'

'Why are you shouting?'

'I'm not shouting. I'm just trying to tell you that if she comes to dinner something terrible will happen.'

'Like what?'

'I don't know. But it will.'

'So tell Dad.'

'Tell him what?'

'I don't know. That's what I was asking you.'

I sat on the landing halfway up the stairs. The smell of fried onion and roasting chicken wafted up from the kitchen. My father was an inventive cook who very occasionally created astonishing, and often somewhat unusual, dishes from whatever he could lay his hands on. My mother provided us with delicious, nutritious, perfectly balanced meals throughout our childhood and adolescence, but of course the only meals I remember with any clarity are the few that my father made.

Max came out of his room and joined me on the landing. 'That black stuff has run down your face.'

'It's called mascara, you cretin.'

He sat down next to me and sniffed at the pungent air. 'It's going to be one of Dad's extravaganzas. Let's hope she likes experimental cuisine.'

'She can't come here.'

'So explain what's wrong,' Max said gently, wiping my cheek with his thumb.

'I can't.'

'Just tell him – and then it'll be OK.'

'Don't be stupid.'

'Dad!' he called out. 'Julia's got something to say to you.'

'Shut up, idiot.'

'Dad! Come here a minute.'

'What's the matter now?' asked my father, peering up the stairs and wiping his hands on his apron. There were beads of sweat on his forehead and one or two pieces of onion skin in his hair.

'You've got to tell Mum,' I said.

'Tell Mum what?'

'When she comes back. You've got to tell her that Sister Collins came here for dinner while she was away. You've got to tell her. Or if you don't, I'll have to, and that would be much worse.'

My mother would joke that she could always tell what I was worrying about just by lifting up my fringe and looking at my forehead. Sometimes, when I was younger and I desperately wanted to talk to her about something but was too upset or embarrassed, I'd beg her to lift up my fringe and try to guess what was wrong. She always got it right, and I loved the tremendous rush of relief and absolution that her guessing engendered. I knew that she would only have to look at me – she wouldn't even need to lift up my fringe – to know that I had been a party to this betrayal.

My father rolled his eyes heavenwards.

'All right, all right, dear. I'll tell your mother. What is all this nonsense about? Now go and lay the table, could you? We'll need soup spoons.'

And with that he poured himself a drink, walked back into the kitchen and shut the door.

A couple of hours later, my father called us down for dinner. One table setting had been removed. He began serving up the soup. It was green with bits of bacon and parsley and something else, as yet unidentifiable, floating in it.

'Where's your guest?' asked Max.

'What, dear?'

'Sister Collins. Where is she?'

'Oh, she rang a while ago. There's been some kind of problem with her parents and she's had to go to see them in Camberley.'

Max and I looked at each other. The telephone hadn't rung at all during the afternoon. I knew that, as I'd been waiting for a call from a boy I'd briefly, but quite successfully, snogged at a recent Venture Scouts disco. We ate the meal in silence. Max washed up, I dried and my father sat in his study and finished off a bottle of whisky.

And, though there was nothing to tell my mother on her return, it was a nothing that felt to me like a suspended sentence. It would all end in tears – I had absolutely no doubt of that. It was only a matter of time.

# VI

I think I was about thirteen or fourteen the first time our house was hit by one of those phosphorus bombs. And it got stuck in the rafters above my bedroom and the roof caught fire. My mother and I ran out of the shelter at the bottom of the garden and we started getting buckets of water and sand and ladders and some of the neighbours came to help. And at some point, I glanced round and I saw my father standing in the garden, looking up at his house. Standing there in his lambswool dressing gown and maroon leather slippers. And I shouted, 'Get some water – quick!' and he just stood there staring up at the house and did absolutely nothing. I went up to him – I was shouting at him to help. Screaming and swearing at him. I didn't care if he hit me. I didn't care *what* he did to me. And then I smelt this terrible smell and it wasn't the smell of something burning. It was a different kind of awful stench and I saw that he was literally shitting himself. He was standing there in his lambswool dressing gown and leather slippers and shitting himself. And at that moment I saw him for what he really was. That bully – that man who beat me and my mother, who ruled our lives like some medieval tyrant – like some almighty *dictator* – was nothing but a terrified little coward. And when we finally put the fire out – my mother and me and the SS man from up the road and eventually the fire brigade – all my books were burned. Every single one of them.

*And how did you feel about that?*

How did I feel? About the burned books?

*About the way your father did nothing to help you? Did nothing to protect you?*

When did he ever do anything for me? I didn't expect him to protect me. I expected him to get a bucket of water and help us put the fire out and not stand there crying and shitting himself as he watched his precious house going up in flames.

*But wouldn't you have liked to feel protected?*

How would I have known what that felt like?

*So you've never felt it?*

Felt what?

*Protected. Cared for. Loved.*

My mother loved me.

*Apart from her.*

Not really. Once, maybe. Quite a long time ago.

*Do you want to talk about it?*

No. Not particularly. Do you want to hear about it?

*If you want to talk about it.*

He was a piano teacher.

*When you were a child?*

No. Not when I was a child. A few years ago. Seven. Eight. I don't know.

*And could you have been happy with him? This piano teacher who loved you? Who could have protected you?*

I very much doubt it. I didn't deserve him. It could never have worked. And anyway, I'll never know. So what's the point of even thinking about it?

*Did you think of marrying him?*

I was already married.

*Was he?*

No.

*Did you think about divorcing your husband and marrying the piano teacher?*

No.

*You didn't think about it?*

No.

*Did anyone else know about him?*

What about him?

*About you and him?*

There never was a me and him. And no, they didn't.

*But your children love you.*

I told you I don't want to talk about them here. With you. They're not part of all this.

*Aren't they?*

Of course they're not.

*Do they know you come here?*

Who?

*Your children.*

No.

*Do they know about the things you've told me?*

Are you crazy?

*Do they know any of it?*

No.

*What do you think would happen if they did know?*

They never will.

*They'd still love you.*

Just stop.

*What do you think would happen?*

Just stop. Now.

*Do you think your children would think you were the enemy?*

Have you gone deaf?

*What?*

I said stop. I said don't talk about my children. They're not part of all this.

*Aren't they?*

# Chapter Seven

My bedroom – Catherine's now – is directly above my father's study. He and I shared the same view of the garden and fishpond during the long summer evenings while I sat on my windowsill reading and he sat at his desk doing whatever it was he did in his study. Throughout my childhood, I assumed that sitting in the study with the door shut was how everyone's father spent their evenings. It never occurred to me that some fathers might do something else, or even that houses without studies might exist.

Of course, I had some insights into the world outside. I knew that there were things called pubs. They were places to which my mother sometimes gave workmen a lift after they had spent a day at our house laying the terrace or installing new light fittings. For years I thought that only men in blue overalls with blunt pencils behind their ears and tattoos of bleeding hearts on their forearms were allowed to go into them.

I knew, too, that there were cinemas. Max and I would sometimes go to the local Odeon with its scratchy red seats, its sticky floor, its smell of stale cigarette smoke and motes of dust dancing in the light of the projector.

'The man sitting next to me has got his hand on my leg,' I hissed to Max once, during one of our outings.

'So?'

'So change places with me. Quick!'

'I like this seat.'

When the hand started inching from my left knee towards my groin, I stood up, avoiding eye contact with my neighbour, and squeezed past Max to sit on his other side. After a short delay, the man moved to the row behind us and sat breathing heavily in my ear for a while before tiring of the pursuit and leaving the cinema, his plastic bags rustling with disappointment as he departed.

'He was probably just a bit lonely,' suggested Max as we walked the mile back to Eynsford Park. 'It can't be much fun going to the cinema on your own.'

So we knew there were cinemas, but we didn't know that they were places to which one's parents might ever think of going with each other, just for fun.

'Do you remember the hideous Olivier of Rennes?' I asked Max once – just after he moved to Dorset, I think.

'Your French exchange's brother? Who used to stick his tongue down your throat while muttering "pussicett, pussicett"?'

'That's the one.'

'I remember you telling me about him. I always wondered how he did that. Perhaps he became a ventriloquist in later life. Had a very successful career on stage and screen.'

'He became a gynaecologist.'

'Oh. Well, I suppose that makes sense. I didn't know you were still in touch.'

'We're not. I made that bit up. About the gynaecology, not the kissing. And there never was an exchange the other way, remember? I stopped replying to Marie-Solange's letters. I told Mum she'd dropped English. I just couldn't face her coming to stay with us and seeing Dad stumble about the house, spilling whisky down his tie. And anyway, she'd only have fallen in love with you and gone all pathetic, like the rest of my friends.'

Max smiled and shook his head.

'You're mad.'

'Don't try to tell me you don't remember how they used to wait for you at the station and then pretend they lived on the estate, just so that they could walk home with you?'

'That only happened once or twice.'

'Once or twice a month, you mean. But you know what amazed me more than the feeling of his tongue against my tonsils?'

'Whose tongue?'

'Olivier of Rennes' tongue. Keep up.'

'I'm not even going to try to guess.'

'It was his parents.'

'God! What did they do?'

'No, no. Nothing like that.'

'Well, that's a relief!'

'One evening, Monsieur Fournier came home from work, changed out of his suit and strolled off arm in arm with Madame Fournier to the cinema, just the two of them.'

'And then what?'

'Nothing. That was it. That was the moment I realised that some people's parents did things together. You know, they never went anywhere, just the two of them. Just for fun.'

'I thought you just said that's what they did.'

'Not the Fourniers, idiot. Mum and Dad.'

'So?'

'So don't you think that was odd?'

'Not really.'

'What? Never once for one of them to have said, "Come on, let's go to the cinema," or "Let's go for a walk," or something.'

'Wandering round and round the cul-de-sacs of Eynsford Park Estate, with dozens of pairs of eyes staring at you from between the spider plants and net curtains, probably wouldn't have been that much fun.'

'Well, you know what I mean.'

'Maybe people didn't go out as much. In those days.'

'In those days! It was the 1960s, for God's sake!'

The '60s must have been going on all around us (I've seen the old news footage) but the revolutionary decade seemed to bypass our corner of Tenterden Close. At some point my father discarded his white shirts, progressing cautiously via striped shirts with white collars to pastel blue or green ones, but apart from that he took no part in the heady fashion revolution. A weekend might be signalled by the donning of a grey cardigan, but never the removal of a tie.

There are almost no photographs of my mother from that time. The few that exist show a slim young woman, smiling reluctantly with her mouth closed or holding up her hand to deflect the camera's gaze. Her hair is back-combed, her dresses knee-length. The pictures are black and white, but I'm pretty sure that most of the dresses are various shades of blue. I am certain, however, that there is not a false eyelash, string of big plastic beads or floppy purple velvet hat in any of them. And as for Love and Peace and all that, I don't remember much of it going on in our house. At least not after Roland went away.

Catherine's bed is in the same position as mine used to be, the headboard under the window, one side pushed up against the wall. I move her rumpled combat trousers, a large pink teddy bear and a notebook with gilt lock and fluffy red cover to the end of the bed. Then, like Goldilocks, but older and greyer and less inclined to compare the quality of the furniture, I lie down and shut my eyes.

We have been driving for hours and hours. My bare legs are sticking to the plastic seat; my plaits are damp with sweat. Insects splat against the windscreen, leaving trails of pale pink blood and creamy entrails. My father switches on the wipers and the viscera are marshalled to either side of the glass. The hedges are high, the roads narrow.

'Slow down,' says my mother grimly from time to time, gripping the edge of her seat.

'Yes, dear,' replies my father.

I see the needle of the speedometer move slightly to the right, not the left, and am relieved that my mother is staring at the road ahead.

'Carry on, then,' I say to Max.

For the past couple of hours, Max and a piece of used grey chewing gum fashioned into a small insect-like creature have been entertaining me with their extraordinary adventures. Eddie Flea has been out on raids with the head-hunters of Borneo, has clung on between the horns of an angry bull in the grandest bull ring of Madrid, has sneaked into *Apollo 11* and landed on the moon, undetected by Neil Armstrong and his fellow astronauts.

'And now,' continues Max, holding the piece of gum above his head, 'Eddie Flea's plane is landing at Heathrow, his adventures finally over. The landing is smooth. Everyone applauds. Eddie is the first off the plane.'

Max walks the piece of gum up his leg towards the hem of his grey shorts.

'He stands at the carousel waiting for his teeny little rucksack to appear. Then, just as he steps forward to pick it up, someone treads on him.'

'What?'

Max squeezes the piece of gum between his thumb and forefinger. 'Someone treads on him and that is the end of Eddie Flea.'

'You can't do that! Bring him to life again.'

'Poor Eddie Flea is as flat as a pancake and dead as a dodo. And that's the end of the story. For ever and ever. Amen.'

'No, it isn't! That's not fair, Max. Make him recover.'

'I'm afraid that's impossible.' Max opens the window and throws the broken body on to the road. 'Eddie Flea is no more.'

I shove my elbow into his ribs very hard.

'Ouch! What did you do that for?'

'What's the matter now?' sighs my father.

And then we are driving up a narrow farm track. Two small brown and white dogs come rushing towards the car. They race behind it up to the house. One of them has only three legs but it's still pretty fast. As the track widens into a courtyard, they tear round and round the car, snapping at the tyres.

'Watch out for the dogs!' I scream.

My father is not a lover of animals. He is not someone who swerves to avoid squirrels and pheasants. Or even cats. When he switches the engine off, I open the door with my eyes squeezed tight, my ears buzzing with fear, dreading the sight of the bloody, smashed bodies. But when I cautiously open my eyes are the little brown and white dogs, barking and lunging at us like over-enthusiastic fencers. The door of the farmhouse opens and the dogs dash in past a woman who strides out towards us, a toddler on her shoulders. She is tall and lean, with long, wavy brown hair, some strands of which are tied back with an eclectic collection of clips, combs and multicoloured ribbons. She is wearing faded, frayed jeans and what look to me like layers of coloured blouses under an embroidered waistcoat. Around her wrists are silver bangles. She smiles at my father – a smile so warm and so wide that, for a moment, her dark brown eyes disappear completely. She swings the toddler to the ground. Then she puts her jangling arms around my father and kisses him on the cheek.

'I'm Jane,' she says to my mother, holding out her hand. 'It's lovely to meet you at last.'

We sit at a long wooden kitchen table. The toddler sits on my father's lap, one arm wrapped round his neck, fondling my father's left earlobe. With its other hand, it is fishing for crumbs in the deep cracks in the table with a fork. One of the little dogs jumps on to the table and pinches a piece of fruit cake. Two more children join us. One looks about the same age as me, the other a little younger. I think they are both boys but it's hard to tell. They each have long curly brown hair and their faces are suntanned and streaked with mud. The younger one seems to be wearing a man's shirt over his ragged jeans, all the buttons done up in the wrong holes. The older one stands behind his mother, resting his chin on her shoulder. They look so alike, with their dark eyes and high cheekbones, that I find myself smiling. They smile back at me.

'Do you want to come and play with us?' the child standing behind his mother asks.

I glance at my mother, who is sitting at the far end of the table watching my father with the small child. I wish – just one little wish – that she would turn and look at me and smile, and say brightly, 'Off you go and have a good time, darling,' but I know that she doesn't want me to go, and I feel that familiar sensation of being slowly torn in two. Love, pity and a biting rage begin to seep through me as I resign myself to staying in the kitchen to protect my mother from whatever it is that's troubling her.

'Good idea, darling!' says Jane, smiling. 'Off you all go – and take some cake with you if you like.'

I don't let myself look in the direction of my mother again.

'What are your names?' the older child asks as we walk through the low-ceilinged passage into the sunny sitting room, munching on fruit cake.

'Julia. And he's Max.'

'I'm Jolyon and this is Ivo. The little one's Octavia.'

'Is that a boy or a girl?' asks Max.

'A girl. It means the eighth but she's just the third. I don't think Mummy's going to have any more now. But you never know. Jamie is quite keen, I think.'

'Who's Jamie?'

'Octavia's daddy.'

'I thought she was your sister.'

'She is. But our daddy's called Matthew. He comes here all the time with his other children. They're younger than me and Ivo. They're called Sebastian and Flora. That means flower. What does your name mean?'

'I don't know. Nothing, I think.'

'How old are you?' asks Jolyon.

'Twelve,' says Max.

'Nearly ten,' I say.

'I'm eight and three-quarters and Ivo's seven next Tuesday. She's in love with Oscar,' says Jolyon matter-of-factly as he throws himself into the huge worn sofa.

'Who is?' I ask, confused as much by the unexpected use of my father's name as by the thought of anyone being in love with him.

'Octavia is. She loves him. Jane says Octavia probably knows that Oscar saved her life. Even though she's so little.'

'She would have died at least three times if it hadn't been for Oscar,' says Ivo authoritatively as he (I'm pretty sure by now that he is a he) flicks through a pile of LPs. 'Jane said, once he drove out to the hospital twice in the same night to save her. Did you know that?'

'No,' I say.

Max, Jolyon and Ivo sit on the floor and play a game involving a pile of pointed sticks with different-coloured stripes on them. I lie on the sofa listening to the record that Ivo has put on. The music is like nothing I have ever heard before. It fills me with a sense of longing for something I cannot recognise, but which seems almost within my grasp.

I look around the room. The walls are covered with huge black and white photographs. There is one of Jane – completely naked – by a waterfall, holding a small bare child by the hand. The child is clutching his penis – both of them are grinning at the camera. There is a picture of Jane and a man with a large scar over his right eye and down his cheek in bed, their hair tousled, their smiles drowsy, the sheets rumpled. There are photographs of Jane and her children with people who look vaguely familiar. One of them is wearing a pair of little round metal-framed glasses. I think he might be John Lennon. I'm pretty sure another of them is Peter Sellers on the set of a *Pink Panther* film. He is holding a little boy – I think it's Jolyon – by the hand and rolling his eyes heavenwards. Jolyon is leaning against his leg, laughing. There is a photograph of Jane bending over a hospital cot in which a tiny baby lies on its back, its face and body covered in plastic tubes, valves and sticky tape. A hand is resting on its swollen belly. I recognise my father's fingers. Pinned to the sitting room door are sheets of stamps and pages torn from a spiral notebook on which messages are scrawled in generously swirling purple ink: *Jolyon and Ivo to Matt and Molly on 25th*; *Octavia to physio 30th*; *plane tickets – Cannes*; *pony to farrier Monday*.

And it feels as though I have entered a different world. A world where absolutely anything could happen. A world where people stand naked under waterfalls; where they talk and laugh and love each other, and each other's children; where people sing of couples making love up in their bedrooms and bridges over troubled water; where chattering children lie on the floor and play, their filthy bare feet waving in the air; where strangers are welcomed with hugs and kisses and cake; where a little brown and white dog with three legs can run like the wind. And now that I have gone through the door, into this other world, I don't ever want to go back.

Caroline Statham didn't believe me when I told her about Jane Bentall.

'You can't have met her! I don't believe you.'

'I have. I promise.'

'Liar!'

'I have! We went to her farm. At half-term. She invited us.'

'Where is it, then?'

'I don't know. Somewhere in the country.'

'Why would she invite you to her farm? And why would a film star live on a farm anyway?'

'I don't know. But she does. We stayed for tea.'

'Mum! Julia says she's met Jane Bentall.'

'Really?' said Mrs Statham spooning spaghetti hoops on to thin slices of white toast cut into triangles, the crusts neatly removed. 'I saw her at the Odeon just the other day. On the screen, I mean, of course. Not actually in the cinema. She used to be married to that good-looking actor who was in all those action films with a twist, wasn't she? Whatsisname. Matthew Someone-or-other. Quite a pair they were, by all accounts. There used to be lots in the papers about them – the parties they had, and everything. All jolly racy. And she was in that French film without her top on.'

'Mum!'

'Well, it was quite something. Everyone went to see it. There was rather a hoo-hah about it at the time. People said it was art, but I don't know. Your father went to see it twice, Caroline, and he's not even all that keen on the cinema! Are two pieces of toast enough for you, Julia?'

'Yes, thanks.'

'So how come you know Jane Bentall?'

'My dad operated on one of her children.'

'He's a clever man, your father. But then, so many of them are. Worcester sauce, girls?'

So it can't have been true – what I said to Max. That we spent our childhood not knowing that there were other ways of being. That my eyes were first opened the summer of the Fourniers. They were opened long before that – on the day we went to Jane Bentall's farm.

# VII

What do you think we did? Pull the heads off chickens?
Ferret out Jewish families from Berlin's attics and cellars
and parade them through the streets with placards round
their necks? Spend our days manufacturing little yellow
stars? What do you think we did? We marched, we sang, we
camped, we kept fit, we searched through burning rubble for
survivors after bombing raids, we kept our uniforms smart,
we had fun. What do you want me to say? That we all knew?
What did we know? We knew nothing. Okay, yes, we knew
there was some kind of prison in Oranienburg. It was for
political prisoners, we were told. Did I wonder why those
Jews were leaving – the ones my mother helped – and where
they were going? I don't think I did. Is that such a crime? Is
that such a terrible thing? What do *you* think goes on in that
big house across the road with the very small brass plaque on
the door? Come on – you sit here every day gazing out of the
window – you must know. You go in and out of this house
every day. You must know what's happening over there. It's
just across the road. But you don't, do you? Have you ever
even read what's on the plaque?

*It's a dental practice, I think.*

You think. But you don't know. And if it says it's a dentist, is
it really a dentist? And where's that tramp who used to sit on
that bench in the square? You know, the one who mumbled
and dribbled and generally made the place look untidy? You

can't say you never noticed him. Where's he gone? To another bench, you assume, but have you asked anyone? Have you ever wondered whether he's all right – if he perhaps needs medical attention, or a decent meal? Where do the gypsies go when the police move them on from the common? You don't know, do you? You drive past the common every day but it's not your problem, is it? Someone else is in charge of all that. And there are rules about how people have to be treated so they must be all right, all those missing gypsies and tramps, mustn't they? The council has procedures. No one beats up or kills people like that – it's not allowed, is it? They're all bound to be fine. They're just not here.

*Why are you so angry?*

It's all right for children to be told about Father Christmas, isn't it? And the tooth fairy. By people they trust? People they look up to? Well, isn't it?

*Yes. I suppose it is.*

And then, when the child grows up, it's all right to for the child to say, 'Well, I believed in Father Christmas and the tooth fairy absolutely and thought they were marvellous, but then when I got a bit older I realised it wasn't true and I moved on.'

*Yes.*

And no one thinks any worse of them for having once been persuaded to believe in a lie. They're not damned for life, and never allowed to be forgiven, for having once believed the lie. I was chosen to present flowers to Hitler on one occasion. There! I knew you'd be impressed.

*Go on.*

You know, there is not a single photograph of me as a child. If any were ever taken – and I don't even know if any were

– they were all destroyed during the war. Then, a couple of years ago there was an article in the *Observer*. Celebrating the life and work of some photographer or other. And there I was. There *we* were. The Führer bending down to receive the garland, and me – blonde-haired, blue-eyed, straight-backed – beaming up at him.

*That must have been a shock.*

I went to Rommel's state funeral and there weren't many young people invited. It was a great honour. I remember everything about it. It was an incredibly big, sad occasion – a hero's funeral. And there he was, lying in state with this magnificent eulogy about how he'd died a hero from wounds sustained in action in Africa, and there was a huge wreath from Hitler and everything. And then in 1945 all those secrets and lies were exposed and I found out that Rommel hadn't been killed in action and that the state funeral had been a total charade. He had turned against Hitler and one of Hitler's cronies had given him a pistol and said if you shoot yourself and go quietly we won't shoot your wife and son. And so Rommel shot himself and got a state funeral. Lies. All lies. And I believed them all.

# Chapter Eight

I open my eyes, and for a second or two I see the green and cream spines of the children's encyclopaedias that I used to open at random and read in bed while waiting for my mother to come home from her woodwork evening class. Martin Luther King; Bedlingham Terrier; Volcano; Pluto; Karl Marx; Dubrovnik. For much of my school career, my general knowledge was legendary. If my school had ever entered a team for *Top of the Form*, with me at the helm, we'd have walked it.

I don't know any more why it seemed so important to wait up to see my mother when she got home. Perhaps I hoped that the contentment she had discovered through transforming pieces of wood into tables, magazine racks and bookshelves would last the journey home; that when she came up to kiss me goodnight, a vestige of that happiness would somehow permeate into me.

When I could no longer keep my eyes from closing, I'd get out of bed and arrange the encyclopaedias into complex geometrical patterns across the floor, then attempt to traverse the room without touching the carpet. As soon as I heard my mother's car drawing up in the drive, I'd quickly gather up the books, put them back in alphabetical order and get into bed to wait for her. But I hardly ever managed to stay awake long enough to kiss her or breathe in the smell of teak oil and wood-shavings. I'd fall asleep the moment I heard the front door open.

I look at my watch. I still have a bit of time left. I swing my feet over the edge of the bed and stand up. It feels as though it should be dark outside, but the sun is still shining. I smooth the outline of my body from Catherine's bedspread, put her things back where I found them, and walk out into the corridor. Judging from the *Thomas the Tank Engine* stickers on the door, the room next to Catherine's must now be Ben's. Our neighbours in the Close would probably have called this the guest room, but in our house, where no guests stayed long enough to require a bed, it was very definitely the spare room. My grandmother stayed in it when she came to see us every few months, but I never felt that she really counted as a guest.

My father would telephone his mother every Sunday evening and sometimes, while hovering outside his study, clutching whatever piece of homework I needed him to do for me, I'd listen to the stories he'd tell her. They were stories of a family that sounded quite a bit like ours – the children (who were doing extremely well with their piano and violin lessons, their swimming, schoolwork and drama productions) were even called Max and Julia. But, in the family that my father spoke of, there was very definitely no mother who sometimes disappeared into the night, deaf to the howling and pleading of her frightened children; no father who had cigarette burns in all his grey cardigans and whisky stains on all his ties, whose hand sometimes shook so violently that the golden liquid sloshed on to the carpet; no son who finished his violin practice and then crept into his cupboard to sleep; no daughter who hurled her maths books across her father's study in rage and frustration.

I remember my grandmother's departures more than her arrivals. My father would drive her to London to catch the train back to Oxford and Max and I would drift quietly through the house, hoping that our mother would have stopped crying before he returned. We couldn't understand why our grandmother upset her so much and so often. We knew that she could say hurtful things: 'Julia – take off those glasses before I take your photo. You look so ugly,' was one comment that I remember particularly clearly. We learned to ignore most of her wounding observations, something my mother never did.

I loved my lone visits to my grandmother's house where, liberated from the responsibility of protecting my mother from her mother-in-law's critical gaze and razor-sharp tongue, I was free to enjoy the thick goose-down quilts, the breakfasts of soft boiled eggs and tinned sardines mashed up in a tea cup, the smell of fresh coffee, the kilner jars of exotic vegetables in her larder, the sumptuous Turkish carpets, the treasures from her travels throughout the world that adorned the sitting room. And her stories.

*In former times…* she would start, her English fluent and precise, her accent thick as goose-fat. If I sat quietly enough, sipping my cocoa and nodding occasionally, she would continue for several hours. These were stories she had told many, many times, and she would repeat them practically word for word, as though reciting a kind of twentieth-century epic poem.

*Your great–grandfather, he had the first car in the city. He was by then already a very famous man. The first thing I remember him saying to me – it was 1898 – 'Clara, when you grow up you will be a doctor.' And so that is what I did. And when he founded the medical school, I was the first person to be enrolled. Nineteen hundred fourteen. We were mostly girls, for the men they were all in the war.*

Sometimes we would look through her photograph albums together.

*Let me see,* she would say, lifting up the crisp semi-opaque paper that protected the pictures. *Ah, yes, that is your father on a school trip, sitting outside a museum. See that? All the public buildings had flags with swastikas on them at that time.*

He was then about nine years old. That must have been about a year before we left Germany. And here is your father sitting on the boxes. November nineteen hundred thirty-six. And then the packers came. We had been told that the import of wine into Turkey was prohibited. When I returned from town that day, I was surprised that not all the linen had fitted into the large laundry box. When I questioned the packers about this, I got the reply – if you ask stupid questions, you will get stupid answers. Imagine how happy we were in Ankara when we found in the lower part of the box not laundry but wine, and moreover the best of the wine. How we drank to the health of those packers.

And you know when we arrived in Turkey, your father's teacher, Herr Schmidt, sent letters from all his class friends explaining what they were learning in case we couldn't find a good school in Ankara. He was a very upright man, this Herr Schmidt. A good man among so many bad. Later we heard he had been killed directly at the start of the war.

And this, this is our house in Ankara. You see how primitive that country was then. Shortly after we arrived, our cook, Eva, wrote to us and told us she had decided to come to Turkey to join us. Here she is, standing in our kitchen. Look how terribly fat she is! Just like a fat pig. And then we discovered that your father had written to her saying we were all being looked after badly and not eating well, so she must come. For cooking was not something I did in former times. I had far too many more important things to do than cook. So Eva came and your father would spend hours with her in the kitchen, learning how to cook vegetables we had never seen before, like aubergines and courgettes. He was very happy at that time, your father. He loved to cook. And he loved Eva. And Eva, she adored him too. But she did not like the Turks. To her they were all dirty and uneducated and she didn't care that we had so many very important Turks visiting us who were so very obviously not dirty or uneducated. And Eva, *she was allowed to go for coffee at the German embassy on Sunday afternoons where the ambassador's daughter gave coffee parties for all the employees of German families. But then, one day, Eva was told that she could no longer go to those coffee parties if she continued to work for us and was told that people might make difficulties for her if she wanted to return to Germany. Therefore we decided to send her back. She did not want to go, but we insisted. She travelled back to Germany on a freighter ship and this was the greatest experience of her life. After her came Miss Krug, supposedly from the German-speaking part of Switzerland, who turned out to be a Nazi spy and who reported every German who came to our house – and at that time we still had many German friends who were not Nazis – to the Blockwart who had been appointed by the Nazis for our part of the city to keep an eye on the German expatriates. We dismissed her immediately when we found out. Then we had a Turkish servant, Cemil, who had already been trained very well by the Zuckmeyers. He became a perfect cook. For large parties, which we very often gave, he would cook and dish up and serve, and he never broke a single piece of my Meissen china. Unfortunately, after we left, he died, like all his family, of tuberculosis. The Fellners, who had inherited him from us, were very disappointed to lose such a cook. Here, and this is our country house in Bavaria. And that is our peasant, Hans, who worked in the garden.*

*And there is your father with his private tutor, Frau Mehmet. She was a most marvellous teacher – a German married to a Turk. But then in 1939 we decided to send your father to England so that he could attend a really good school there. For he was such a very clever boy and the schools in Turkey were not so good at that time.*

*But we had not expected that it would be nearly seven years before we would see him again.*

'What, dear?' said my father when I asked him to tell me about his time at boarding school. And then he changed the subject. I never even found out the name of his school.

In my early teens, I went through a brief period of steaming open my parents' letters. I think we must have been shown how to do it on *Blue Peter*. Sadly we weren't told how to re-seal them, but I don't think my parents ever suspected me of tampering with their post. Mostly the contents of their envelopes were pretty dull – bills, advertisements, samples from drug companies. Sometimes there would be letters to my father from grateful patients, often containing childish drawings that he would leave on his desk for a day or two propped up against his reading lamp before throwing them in the bin.

Then, one Saturday morning when I came down to pick up the post, hoping for a letter from my good-looking Mexican pen-friend, I found an airmail envelope with a Spanish stamp on it, addressed to my father. I turned it over. There was an address – just a PO Box and a Spanish city – on the back of the envelope. There was no sign of anyone else at home so I took it to the kitchen, held it over the boiling kettle and opened it very carefully. Inside were several small sheets of flimsy blue stationery, covered in neat italic writing in black ink.

Curious, I carried the letter up to my bedroom and lay on the bed. The letter started without a salutation, as though, unable to decide how to address my father, the writer had decided not to call him *Dear* anything.

*Last month I was back in England for medical treatment – I run a property business in southern Spain – and found myself watching a documentary about surgeons at a London teaching hospital carrying out some ground-breaking new surgical technique. This is not something I would do under normal circumstances, but since being diagnosed with cancer of the oesophagus I have had a morbid curiosity about all things medical. When one of the surgeons spoke, the voice was somehow familiar, though all I could see was a pair of eyes peering at the bloody mess on the operating table. Then the narrator mentioned you by name and I immediately knew exactly who it was behind the green mask.*

*You may remember me – in fact, I fear that there is little chance you could have forgotten me. Though I doubt you ever knew my Christian name. What we did to you during those years at Massingham was, and is, not condonable. All I can say in my – in our – defence is that it was poor timing. Those war years were a bad time to be a Jew with a German accent at a second-rate Methodist public boarding school in rural Suffolk. If you had excelled at rugby or fives rather than biology and chemistry, if you had challenged us, if you had resisted, maybe there would have been some hope for you. Maybe every day wouldn't have been such torture. But I doubt it. We were a cruel lot. Someone should have noticed what was going on and put a stop to it, but the masters were little better than we were. There was just Mr Creighton, but we soon got rid of him. A few whispers in the right ears and he was gone. I doubt he ever got another teaching position. He was a good, kind, man who tried to do the right thing and deserved better than an ignominious dismissal.*

*That you have clearly done so well and been so successful in your chosen career is a source of great pleasure and, dare I say it, relief. After that documentary, I made some discreet enquiries and learned that you are married with children. That, too, gives me pleasure. But it does not give me absolution – only you can do that. I do not deserve it, but I ask for*

*your forgiveness. It is the pathetic plea of a dying man.*
*I live in hope of hearing from you.*
    *Yours,*
        *Eric Long*

I read the letter again and again, committing the terrible words to memory. My hands shook as I folded the sheets of paper and pushed them back into the envelope. The stamp was curling up at the edges. I pressed hard on to the corners. I could feel my pulse pounding in my thumb. I got out my tub of almond-smelling glue and pasted the envelope shut. Then I went downstairs and slid it between two ordinary-looking brown envelopes on my father's desk.

That evening, when I went into his study with my algebra homework, I saw the blue pages lying on the desk. He was holding the envelope in his hand, just staring at it.

'That's a nice stamp,' I said as casually as I was able to. 'Where's it from?'

'Spain, I think.'

'Can I have it for school? We collect them for guide dogs.'

'I don't think it'll be much good for that. It's rather ragged at the edges.'

'Who do you know in Spain?'

'No one.'

'So who's it from, then?'

'What, dear?'

'Who's it from?'

'Just someone I was at school with.'

'Who lives in Spain now?'

'Seemingly.'

'That's nice.' I wondered if my father could hear my voice shaking. 'Are you going to write back?'

Without saying anything, my father put down the envelope, collected up the sheets of notepaper, and slowly tore them into tiny pieces. He did the same to the envelope.

Then he leant over towards his waste-paper bin, held his hand high above it, and let the fragments whirl and eddy into the depths.

'So what's my homework for this evening, dear?' he asked.

# VIII

In my class in Berlin there was a girl who was so obviously different from us – she was very bright, well-educated, very sophisticated. Effie Feldt she was called – and looking back she was so obviously Jewish, a very extrovert Jew. And we became great friends but nobody knew anything much about Effie. She'd joined the school halfway through the term and, although she was very friendly, she kept herself pretty much to herself. Then one day she said, 'Come home for tea with me,' and it was a very big, beautiful house – and she introduced me to her parents who were both university professors and we sat and drank coffee. They were very polite. Polite but a bit distant, I thought. I was surprised at how old they were. Then her parents went out for a walk and I got up and looked at the pictures on the mantelpiece. There was one of her father in an academic gown presenting a certificate to a young man with dark curly hair. And I said, 'What's your father doing in this picture?' And Effie said, 'What do you mean?' in a rather startled way and then came and looked at the picture. And then she said, 'Oh, he's the vice chancellor at the university. He's handing out degree certificates.' And it was only much later that I realised that she was probably the daughter of a Jewish student of the professor's. And it was only much later that I realised that her real parents were probably in a concentration camp somewhere.

*And how did that make you feel?*

Is it important?

*It might be. I don't know.*

I can't remember. How I felt. Stupid, probably.

*Stupid?*

That I hadn't known.

*And if you had known? That this girl was Jewish?*

Would I have been friends with her? Is that what you are trying to say? Or would I have reported her? Is that what you are really trying to say?

*I'm not trying to say anything.*

Of course you are. You sit here, pretending to listen, but you're judging me. You know nothing and here you are, judging me.

*I'm not judging you at all. Go on. Tell me more about Effie Feldt. Please do.*

There's not much more to say.

*Go on.*

I remember one day she said to me, 'You are such a good friend. You are the nicest person I know. I just can't get over the fact that you believe in Hitler.' And I remember saying to her, 'What difference does that make to our friendship?' I was walking down the Kurfürstendamm with her once, and we passed a haberdashers that was all boarded up. If you looked through a crack in the boards you could see hundreds – thousands – of ribbons lying all over the floor – buttons everywhere. I said, 'What a shame about all those lovely ribbons,' and I remember that Effie said, 'Just about the ribbons?' And I didn't know what she meant.

*And did you ever find out what happened to this girl?*

Happened to her?

*After the war?*

I hope she's still alive and perhaps living in Israel or America. That no one ever realised the professors were harbouring a Jew. That they all had the good and long lives they deserved.

*Do you ever think of trying to find her? To get in touch? I'm sure there are ways of doing that. There are lists. Registers.*

And do what then?

*Just rekindle the friendship.*

Are you crazy? Do you think she would want a friendship with me? After all that happened?

*You weren't responsible. We've established that at least, haven't we? She liked you a lot. You were friends.*

Don't talk to me about friendship.

*But don't you think it's important? Friendship?*

Friends have to know you.

*And?*

And if they know you – if they know who you are and who you were and what you were – how can they possibly want to be friends with you?

*Is that what you really think?*

It is.

*So you'd say you have no friends?*

None.

*And you think you can live with no friends? With no one really knowing you?*

I seem to manage.

*Do you?*

I think I do.

*And what about your children?*

They're my children, not my friends. And I told you that I don't want to talk about them here.

*But they would love you even if they knew – who you were, as you put it.*

You really think that?

*I'm sure of it.*

Well, then, you're madder than I've ever been.

*And your husband?*

He knows.

*You told him?*

No. But he knows. He's always known. And he says nothing.

*How do you know? That he knows.*

I see how he looks at me. He knows. And he knows that I know that he knows. And he says – nothing.

# Chapter Nine

I hesitate outside Ben's door, then go back and look into Catherine's room again. I stand in the doorway and try to remember Susanna's bedroom in Dorset. If I shut my eyes I can see her paintings, with their exuberant, watery patterns on rough, cream-coloured paper; her dream-catchers; her hand-woven hangings; her pieces of pottery; her photograph of me with my arm around her on the bedside table that she and Max had made from driftwood, a garland of dried daisies draped around the frame. I think she must have been about eight in that picture. On a visit to Togo. She has Max's wide, generous smile.

I think of my visits to her and Max – two or three times a year, much more often when I came back to live and work in London. It seemed that nearly every time I went, there would be a new foster brother or sister; a visitor who had come for a few days and stayed on for months; a new member of the household; or a woman, invariably sad and beautiful, who thought that maybe – just maybe – she would be the one. I watched Susanna grow and thrive in her chaotic, loving, fluid family, with Max the calm and constant centre, and eventually I stopped begging him to try to persuade her to go back with me to Cameroon or London.

I close Catherine's door and head back towards Ben's room. On the landing is a large framed black and white portrait photograph of the Plaistow family, probably taken a couple of years ago, the six of them arranged artistically over bean bags, the background pure white nothingness. Everyone is smiling at the camera, even the oldest girl who is clearly trying hard not to.

I wonder if a photographer could catch the essence of Max's extensive, ever-shifting family. I doubt it, somehow.

Above Clara's sofa was a massive oil painting of two men standing over an iron cot in which lay a curly-haired infant. Both men were bald. The older one had round, black-rimmed glasses and appeared to be explaining something to the younger man.

'Who are the men in the picture,' I asked once.

'They are your grandfather and your great-grandfather. The picture commemorates the opening of the paediatric hospital my father founded. It is a copy actually, but a good one. You can hardly tell. The original is in the Kunst-Palast – the museum – in Düsseldorf.'

'Crikey!'

'Perhaps I'll take you there one day.'

'So how did you and my grandfather meet? Was it at that hospital?'

*Well, one day, my father brought home his new registrar Arthur Rosenthal. And my father said, Clara, you must make him feel at home here, for by then my mother had already died. So we saw a lot of each other.*

*And then, after some time, my father said to me – that Dr Rosenthal is such a good doctor, the best I have ever seen. I would have to shoot anyone who wanted to marry him and take his interest and attention away from his work. And I said to my father, well, you had better shoot me, then, for Dr Rosenthal and I are engaged. And then he was so delighted – he loved my husband so much. For he was not only a brilliant doctor, he was a most marvellous person. Often my father would say how he loved my husband more than his own son.*

'Who was he?'

'So much interrupting! Who was who?'

'Your father's son?'

'That was my brother Ernst.'

'What happened to him?'

'In former times he was a pharmacist. But he didn't have so much luck, for many different reasons. He too left Germany with his wife, Berthe, but a little later, in 1938, and they went to New York. And then for the next twenty years he pressed the lift buttons in a big department store and went up and down, up and down all day while Berthe made clothes in some sort of a factory. Later she had a little shop in Orchard Street, selling ribbons and buttons, and all those kinds of things.'

'Poor them!'

'Ach, it wasn't so bad. That way they managed to pay for their son Helmuth to go through Harvard, and of course you know what happened to him.'

Though I'd never met Helmuth, I knew he'd become a very eminent economist, frequently quoted in the pages of *Time* magazine. He then made millions in the newly emerging computing business and lived a life of modest plenty just outside Washington DC. My grandmother would occasionally show us photographs of him standing by his pool with his very large wife and four very large all-American children. Beside them, he looked rather small and serious.

*And so, where was I? Ah, yes. We married in nineteen hundred twenty-five and in nineteen hundred twenty-six there came your father. And immediately I got a very excellent wet nurse so I could continue my work, for in those days I no longer practised as a doctor but was in charge of the orphanage. And in any case, in former times, there was not all this nonsense feeding of babies whenever they demanded it. The nursemaid would put your father in his pram at the end of the garden between feeds so neither we nor our visitors* needed to be disturbed by any of his horrible crying. For in former times we had a very big garden. So many times when you and Max were babies, I would say to your mother, 'Put the baby down – all this nonsense picking it up when it cries and carrying it around will spoil the child. Let it cry itself to sleep.' But she never listened.

But then in nineteen hundred thirty-five my husband lost his job in such a depressing and humiliating way. And we knew that it would not be safe to stay much longer in Germany. And then came a phone call from the Foreign Office, which was not yet fully under Nazi domination, that the Turkish Minister of Health was there and was looking for German professors for the hospital in Ankara, so as to promote it into a university hospital. As well as that, the paediatrician was to build up the entire system of infant- and child-care in Turkey – the same task that my father had started for Germany at the turn of the century.

So I was first the daughter of a famous doctor and then I became the wife of a famous doctor and now I am the mother of a famous doctor.

Max had long been marked out to be the next to take on the mantle of medical greatness. *And when you become a doctor...* my grandmother would proclaim as she got out the chessboard and set out the meerschaum pieces. Or, *And when you become a famous doctor...* when she felt particularly proud of her ancestors and descendants. For some reason, I didn't mind that I was never included in this family hall of fame. Max never commented, he just smiled and nodded slightly, but that was enough for my grandmother to feel reassured that the dynasty would continue.

I hated chess, with its endless silences and brooding pawns. My grandmother's efforts to teach me didn't last long.

'It is lucky Max isn't as unintelligent as you,' she observed. 'And your father, when he was only eight, he was chess champion of all the schools in Germany.'

'Big deal,' I muttered.

'You are right,' she said approvingly, unfamiliar with the phrase. 'It was a very big deal and a great honour. So, as you are far too stupid for chess, I had better play with Max. Come, Max, you set up the pieces again. Here, Julia, you can sort out my sewing box while Max and I play. And if you are very quiet, I'll tell you some more family stories later.'

*So, after the breaking off of relations with Germany and the entry of Turkey into war on the Allied side, the members of the German embassy had to leave Turkey. On the day they were being transported away, my husband was called to the commercial attaché, whose child had a very high temperature. He was among the leading Nazis in Turkey and his office was the headquarters of spying. As my husband was about to leave the house, the attaché said to him, 'I thank you for your help – perhaps I can do something for you in Germany – I have influence, if you should have any relatives there.' To which my husband answered, 'They have already been killed, all of them.' Tante Louisa had committed suicide, Sofie had died in Theresienstadt and Renate had been transported away from there to we knew not where and we never heard of her again, though we tried for many years to find out what had happened to her. We were informed exactly by the Jewish Agency what was going on in Auschwitz and elsewhere. The gassing and all the other horrors. The attaché then asked, very embarrassed, for almost no one in Germany knew much about what was going on in Auschwitz or any of the other camps, 'May I ask for your bill?' My husband only said 'Your money is too dirty for me!' and turned his back on him and left.*

Max and I would go to see my grandmother every couple of months, together when we were younger and then separately when my grandmother announced that we were quite old enough to survive the train journey on our own –

*surely we were no longer such little babies?* She was very good at organising people. The first time I went to stay with her on my own, she said, 'Ah, Julia, now you are here as my guest, you can do whatever you like for the next four days. First we will go to the Pitt-Rivers Museum and then we are going to go swimming. And then, after supper, we will look through the photograph albums.'

My mother hated us making the journey to Oxford, though she never tried to stop us. She would stand in the drive, grim-faced, not waving, watching the car drive round the green and out of the cul-de-sac towards the station. She had an unnerving ability to foresee death and destruction in the everyday. If she heard an ambulance's siren just after we left the house for school, she would be filled with an overwhelming sense of doom that would only lift when a few hours had passed without a call from Casualty, or from our schools querying our absence. How we used to laugh at her when she told us about the sirens.

'Why don't you drive us to school, then?' we'd ask, always keen to avoid the long walk and the groups of children from the local primary school who would knock off my grey felt hat and throw Max's navy cap over the privet hedges whenever they got the chance. Why we didn't just carry our hats or shove them into our satchels and avoid this ordeal, I still don't know.

But my mother could rarely pull herself out of bed in the morning before we left for school.

When we arrived in Oxford, one of us would manage to distract our grandmother in the kitchen while the other would creep into the sitting room to ring home and announce our safe arrival. Until we learned to do that, we would be exposed to a line of questioning that always filled me with a deep unease.

'Can I use the phone to ring Mum, please?'

'Is she still so very nervous?'

'Not really. She just likes to know we've arrived safely.'

'And all those medicines she was taking?'

'I don't think she's taking them any more.'

'So perhaps now she is able to look after your father again properly.'

'I think he can look after himself, really.'

'Yes, but if she isn't working, that is something useful she could do, no?'

'She is working, some of the time.'

'Yes, but not in an important job such as your father's.'

'It is, in a way.'

'I can imagine she'll be busy now, preparing your father's supper. He must be so tired when he gets home from the hospital. So phone her quickly and don't talk for long and then we'll eat. And afterwards, Max, you and I will play chess.'

I imagined my mother alone at home, putting down the phone after my call, making my father's supper which would usually be ruined by the time he eventually came home, watching television, wondering what her mother-in-law was saying about her, while Max and I sat in our grandmother's cosy house listening to her stories of 'former times' and eating dumplings, wurst and *rote grütze*.

'Come, Julia. Why the long face? Nothing wrong at home?'

'No, everything's fine.'

My grandmother moved from Germany – where she and her husband had returned some years after the war – to England in the early '60s. She bought a house in what must have once been quite a pleasant, semi-rural area of Oxford not far from two of her favourite second cousins who had been in England since the early 1930s. Very quickly, it was encircled by new streets, houses and flats. Gradually the trim verges began to sprout more litter than grass, the neat curtains in the windows were replaced by pieces of material draped over string, and by the time Max and I were in our teens the little shopping parade opposite the house was deserted apart from a tobacconist's with a permanent grille over the window and a convenience store which boasted a display of brightly coloured plastic fruit and vegetables and little else. Some architectural quirk meant that the parade acted as a wind tunnel, and, every time we went there, plastic bags and chip wrappers would be dancing in the currents of air, lending a festive atmosphere to the otherwise bleak concrete surroundings.

Going shopping with my grandmother was a kind of mild torture. She had a very continental attitude to queuing. Max and I would spend much of our time smiling apologetically at large, fierce-looking women in tight crimplene slacks with cigarettes hanging out of their mouths, or pockmarked teenagers who would find their place in the queue taken by a tall, gaunt, foreigner in her late seventies who appeared not to notice that they existed. If the checkout girls were too slow, my grandmother would declare very loudly, 'Ach, these stupid shop girls! I haven't got so much time to waste,' leave her basket of unchecked-out goods on the end of the conveyor belt and stride out of the shop.

Every day, whatever the weather, my grandmother would swim in the local outdoor pool, only reluctantly going to the indoor sports centre when it closed for the winter months. Until Max and I learned to 'accidentally' leave our swimming things at home, we would reluctantly swim up and down the pool a few times, shivering, while my grandmother, resplendent in a pink bathing cap sprouting yellow rubber flowers, did her twenty lengths. Whenever the bitter winds stopped whipping up ripples on the grey water and the rain clouds cleared, we'd be joined by a handful of other swimmers, who quickly learned to give my grandmother a wide berth as she ploughed up and down, oblivious of any oncoming traffic. Her lengths completed, she would haul herself up the steps, and walk slowly but purposefully to the changing rooms like one of those ancient, wrinkled Galapagos tortoises.

Another of her hobbies to which we'd be recruited was fruit-picking. Each year, she would pick pounds and pounds of strawberries and raspberries or whatever else was in season. Then she would drive to the old people's home near her house and deliver them.

'Ach! They are all so gaga,' she would sigh as she got back into the car. 'They sit around all day staring at the television, even if it is not on. Or playing that stupid English bingo game. If they at least played bridge, their brains would have some exercise and they wouldn't just be sitting there like vegetables. I said that to the matron when I gave her the strawberries.'

'And what did the matron say?' I asked, curious to know how other people dealt with my grandmother.

'I don't know. She had one of those local accents that no one can understand. So I just nodded my head like this and left.'

My grandmother would keep a punnet or two of raspberries and strawberries, which would form the basis of her *rote grütze*. We would watch with some fascination as she emptied the fruit, wriggling maggots and all, into a saucepan and turned it into the delicious pudding which we'd eat with the top of the milk poured over it. We learned not to think about the specks in the pudding that were neither raspberry pips nor strawberry leaves.

*I love to go back to Germany, for there I am a somebody,* my grandmother would say. Each year, she would return to Germany to say goodbye to all her old friends. As the years went by, and more and more of her friends died, Max noted that these by now very old friends probably all dreaded a farewell visit from my grandmother, as it was more likely to presage their own death than hers.

*So many times, I have said, 'Thank God for Hitler,' for if we had not had to leave Germany because of the Nazis and had not gone to Turkey we would not have had all those marvellous times and opportunities and met so many interesting people. For not only was your grandfather in charge of child health throughout the whole of the country, he took over the responsibility for the medical practice of the colony of exiles, and in time also the entire diplomatic corps of the Allies.*

*The children of the German embassy came under his care too as they had greater confidence in a European professor than in a local doctor. It happened very occasionally that a Nazi would prefer to have some other doctor. Only one declared quite openly, 'I would rather have my child die than have it treated by a Jew.' The poor child died soon after, of meningitis, I think.*

I never met my grandfather, Arthur Rosenthal. Clara once said that a colleague of his in Turkey, for whom he had great respect, had told him that people like him should return in order to re-educate the younger generation in Germany. And so they went back to Germany in 1950, where Arthur took up a prestigious university position. Six months later, he died of a heart attack on a picnic aged only fifty-nine, in the same month that my father qualified as a doctor in London. My father kept a photograph of him on his bookshelf. I used to look at my grandfather's kindly face, the smile lines around his eyes, his shiny bald head, and examine him for links to my father or to Max. My father never once spoke about my grandfather and would feign deafness if I ever asked about him.

'Didn't he like him?' I asked my mother once.

'Your grandmother kept your grandfather pretty much to herself as far as I know – I doubt your father ever saw much of him. But I think he loved his father so much, he can't bring himself to talk about him. That's the way your father is – anything difficult or painful, you just don't talk about it.'

I could tell we were heading for dangerous ground here, so I changed the subject.

# IX

I can't tell you how happy I was the time I thought they'd come to take my father away. I was supposed to be meeting my friend Helga at a Furtwängler concert. You've heard of *Kraft durch Freude*? – well, never mind – and I was looking everywhere for the tickets. I couldn't find them anywhere. I was too old now for my father to hit me but he used to find other ways of making my life difficult. Textbooks of mine would go missing and I'd be punished at school, or messages would fail to reach me and I'd miss important meetings or find I'd let my friends down. And suddenly there was a knock on the door and I could see through the glass that it was Herr Schering, who lived with his mother at the end of our street, dressed in his SS uniform. We'd see him go home in the evenings in his black uniform and boots and my mother would say, 'Don't move – the SS man is coming past.' Nobody really spoke to him – and his old mother rarely left the house. I was running incredibly late and still looking for my tickets and I didn't really want to open the door but I thought – finally! They've come to get my father. They've heard him listening to the BBC. So I opened the door and said, 'My father's in the summer house.' But Herr Schering said, 'It's you I wanted to see.' And he said he'd heard that I'd been presented with a medal recently and that I should treasure it forever. And then he asked me if I was just going out somewhere and I told him I was going to the Furtwängler concert but couldn't find my tickets. And he said he'd played with Furtwängler himself. When he'd been a student at the Conservatoire. But that now he didn't have the time to play the French horn as much as he'd like to – there were other, more important things to do. And then he said, 'What's that sticking out of your top pocket?' And there they were. The tickets. And he held out a pair of thick black woollen trousers and said, 'I wondered if you'd have a use for these. They'll need making smaller but I don't need them, I've been issued with another pair and it's a waste to throw them away.' And that's really how I started to sew quite seriously. It was beautiful material. I altered them and made deep pockets with the left-over material and they would have lasted for another twenty years if they hadn't been incinerated. They lasted longer than their original owner, in any case. A couple of weeks later, our SS neighbour came out of his bomb shelter to look at the damage to his house and a roof tile fell on his head and he died. They took his old mother away and I heard she died in hospital shortly afterwards.

# Chapter Ten

Ben's room resembles a small arsenal belonging to someone ready for any means of attack. Scattered over the bright blue carpet are two silver pistols in leather-look holsters, a large machine gun, a gun that fires ping-pong balls, a plastic dagger, a set of wooden swords, some arrows and a broken bow. A naked Action Man lies on the windowsill, its head twisted at an impossible angle, as if recoiling from the sight of its bare rippling muscles and its tiny beige bulge of genitalia.

Max and I used to play cowboys and Indians a lot. He was always the cowboy, and I the Indian. I don't know why that was. Probably because of the lovely long head-dress I got to wear, with its spiky red, yellow and blue feathers. We played in the garden, around our tepee. Playing inside was too risky. Shortly after our grandmother had presented us with the sets of costumes and accompanying weapons, our mother had come into Max's room to call us down for supper. Max had leapt out from behind his curtain where he'd been waiting to ambush me, grabbed her round the neck and held a revolver to her head.

'Hands up!' he yelled.

'Christ almighty!' she shouted, shaking Max off and staggering back towards the wall. We were impressed. She'd got the hang of the game pretty quickly. But then we saw that she was shaking. 'Don't ever do that again, do you hear?' she said, her voice trembling with anger.

'It's just a game, Mum,' said Max, soothingly.

'Just don't ever point a gun at me again. Ever.'

'But it's not real.'

'I don't care. Just don't do it, do you hear me?'

'What about arrows?' I asked, rearranging my head-dress, anxious not to be excluded from the drama.

'What about them?'

'Can we shoot arrows at you?'

'If you must – but from a long distance away and not at my head.'

'But that's not fair,' said Max. 'You tell me off about the gun and then let her shoot you with a bow and arrow. Arrows are just as lethal. Ask any old Indian.'

'Well, that's just how it is.'

'Then I'll shoot myself instead,' he said dramatically, holding the barrel of the gun to his temple.

My mother winced. 'Put the damned thing down!' she shouted.

'It's not loaded,' I protested. 'It's not even got caps in it. We ran out. And anyway, you're always telling us not to swear.'

'Look, I'm sorry. You can keep your guns now that you've got them. I just never want to see them. Ever. And never, ever point one at me. Do you hear?'

It wasn't only guns we had to be careful about. We could make our mother jump out of her skin just by coming up behind her very quietly. As we never wore shoes in the house, this happened a lot. We found it quite funny, watching her literally jump and then clutch her chest as she spun round, but she wasn't at all amused. When we realised that she was far less likely to agree to what we wanted in the aftermath of a shock, we found various ways of heralding our arrival – singing or calling out – as we approached whichever part of the house she was in.

'And is your mother still so very unstable?' our grandmother used to ask, rather too loudly, when she came to stay.

'She's fine,' we'd say, looking round anxiously to check that our mother was out of hearing.

'Such a shame for your poor father.'

'She's *fine*. Really.'

'After all the stress at work and then coming home to all that.'

We didn't really know what 'all that' meant, but we did know it didn't sound fair.

'Mum's all right. And anyway, Dad normally comes home pretty late.'

When I was about thirteen, and after a particularly disastrous visit, my mother told my father that Clara was no longer welcome in our house. Max and I could carry on seeing her whenever we wanted to and so could my father, of course. But Clara was not coming to Tenterden Close ever again.

'But Mum,' I said, 'you can't make Dad do that. It'll hurt Clara's feelings.'

'And what about *my* feelings? Can't there be *one* time when someone thinks about *my* feelings.'

'But she doesn't really mean all the horrible things she says,' said Max. 'They sound worse than they are. It's because she's German.'

My father didn't say anything but he must have passed the message on. I wondered how he fitted the decree into his comfortable family narrative. Max and I continued to visit our grandmother in Oxford, as did my father, but the guest room remained empty, home only to my mother's sewing machine and a dressmaker's dummy we called Natasha. (I think *War and Peace* was on TV at the time.)

My grandmother never mentioned her banishment. It was as if she had never been to stay with us; had only ever entertained us in her own home. Max and I were happy to see her on her own territory where we didn't have to protect our mother from the upset and outrage she caused. My father must have been annoyed at the inconvenience of having to travel to Oxford to see his mother but, if that was the case, he never complained.

My grandmother was interested in nothing as much as 'the Family', by which she meant both her ancestors and descendants and those of her husband. With the help of an elderly and amenable second cousin, she had managed to draw up an immense and highly complicated family tree which went back to Polish rabbis of the seventeenth century. One of my great-uncles claimed Einstein as a relative but, try as I might, I never managed to find him among the hundreds of names.

I'm not sure my history teacher was expecting a chart covering most of one wall when she set us the task of tracing our ancestors as part of a fifth-year genealogy project.

'Are you quite sure that's right?' she asked, squinting up at the chart and pointing to the names three lines above mine and Max's.

'I'm positive it is,' I replied. 'I can't imagine my grandmother making a mistake about her relatives. She's like the Rose Kennedy of the Rosenthals.'

'But your grandmother's mother and aunt were twins.'

'Yes, identical ones. Even their parents couldn't tell them apart. They were legendary.'

'Ah – ' said Miss Harvey. 'And then two of their children married each other.'

'They were cousins – yes. It was very common at the time. For first cousins to marry each other.'

'I see,' said Miss Harvey, looking no less concerned.

When I got home, my mother smiled as I described my teacher's disquiet. 'It's the biology, not the history that Miss Harvey is worried about.'

'What about it?'

'They'd do anything to keep the money in the family, those Rosenthals and Eisensteins. And you wonder why you've got so many mad relatives.'

'I don't!'

'Well, maybe you should. Ask your grandmother about Tante Greta.'

'What about Tante Greta?'

'Her father was one of the leading anatomists of the time. Another of those over-achieving famous men, of course. But when Greta didn't grow properly, he just said, "Well, that's good if she stays small; it'll save buying her new clothes." I bet your grandmother didn't tell you there was a dwarf in the family!'

'Tante Greta wasn't a *dwarf*! I've seen photographs of her. She was just a very small person.'

'Dwarf. Small person. It's all the same.'

'No, it isn't!'

And then there was Tante Käthe. *And here*, my grandmother had said as she helped me copy out her family tree, pointing to a gap in the branches with her gnarled index finger. *Put down Hänsel Eisenstein married Eva Rosen 1905 and they had, in 1907, Erik and in 1910, Hilde, and in 1911, Käthe – but don't bother to write her down.*

I wanted to ask my mother about Tante Käthe, but I couldn't bear the prospect of her triumphant contempt. Nor did I want to hear too many stories of seriously mad blood relatives, particularly those born in the same century as me.

'We're supposed to do both sides of the family,' I told my mother. 'For this history project.'

'Haven't you got enough relatives on your father's side?'

'That's not the point. I need your side too. Just because you're ordinary and English and your parents died when you were quite young, it doesn't mean you're not interesting. It doesn't mean I can just leave you out.'

'I'm really not in the mood to go through all that. Can't you just make it up?'

'Hardly!'

'But that's what you're good at – making up stories.'

'But I can't make up an entire family.'

'I don't see why not.'

And that was that. I never did manage to assemble my mother's family tree. There were no other living relatives on that side, or at least none I'd ever been told of. And so I made up a small dynasty of Croydon railway executives, Merton brewers and Bromley shoe shop owners going back to the 1920s and Miss Harvey gave my efforts an A minus.

# X

My happiest times? I think they were when I was away at my teacher training college which had been evacuated from Berlin to the country. I had finally escaped from my father. There was nothing he could do to me. He paid for me to go. The last thing he wanted was an unemployed cheese head, destined to live at home and be a financial drain on him. As far as he was concerned, the sooner I left and started supporting myself, the better. And the feeling was mutual, I can tell you.

*And what about your mother?*

She stayed with him. Where else could she have gone? But I think he hit her less when I wasn't around. Or maybe she was able to keep out of his way more when she didn't have to be home for me. I think she even stopped making him his meals, which must have annoyed him a lot.

*But you never became a teacher?*

No. History rather saw to that.

*Do you regret it?*

In some ways.

*Do you want to expand at all?*

Not really.

*Does it make you angry? You sound angry.*

Does what make me angry?

*That you weren't able to qualify as a teacher?*

I sometimes wonder if you really hear anything that I'm saying. Anything at all.

*What makes you say that?*

Where were you during the war?

*I was at school. Not far from here. Why?*

Have you never read any books? Never seen any documentaries? Have you any idea what it was like?

*But this isn't about me, is it?*

Have you any idea what it was like? The war?

*I've some idea, of course.*

Then how can you ask me whether the fact that the war stopped me training as a teacher makes me angry? How important are qualifications? The lies are what make me angry. The lies. And the unspeakable cruelty of what one person is capable of doing to another. That's what makes me angry. And the millions of pointless, stupid, unnecessary, terrible deaths. And still feeling like the enemy, all these decades later. Those are the things that make me angry and you might as well stop looking as though you're interested in hearing what I have to say because I don't have anything else to say to you today.

*Well, just think about it. That's all.*

I've got more important things to think about than whether I regret not becoming a teacher.

*Like what?*

Like how I'm going to summon up the energy to get up in the morning. Like how I'm going to keep going. Day after day. Year after year. It's all right. You don't have to look at me like that. I'm not going to kill myself. I've thought about that. That would be far too easy.

# Chapter Eleven

It appears that Anna and Eleanor share the room that used to be Max's. It is dominated by a sturdy pine bunk bed and posters of androgynous boy bands that I vaguely recognise but cannot name. Bisecting the pale pink carpeted floor, from the centre of the base of the bed to the opposite wall is a thick, slightly wobbly chalk line. I wonder what the rules are for crossing it. The resident of the zone on the right is clearly tidier than the one on the left, where pyjamas, notepads, cuddly toys and half-eaten tubes of sweets cover much of the territory.

I lie down on the bottom bunk. On the slats of the bed above me are written the words *Eleanor stinks like a scunk* in blue biro. A little further to the left is a large heart, neatly coloured in with red felt-tip pen. An arrow runs through it with the word 'Anna' at one end and 'Jack' at the other. I see that under 'Jack', but fainter and with angry lines crossed through it, is 'Liam'.

I lie here listening for the sound of the violin but, apart from the ticking of one of the girls' alarm clock, the room is silent.

'You know what they say about violinists?' I asked Max once, sitting down on his bed and idly opening his copy of *Sherlock Holmes*.

'What?' said Max, continuing to play his scales. He could practise for hours at a time and it drove me mad.

'They're all really weird. Violinists. The real loners in an orchestra.'

'That's viola players, actually, if it's stereotypes you're after.'

'Viola players, violinists – they're all the same. The sort of people who are really quiet and stuff and then go and hack the oboists to bits.'

'Oh, yeah?'

'Why don't you listen to Radio Luxembourg like normal people? What's the point of all that scraping away? It sounds like you're grating chalk.'

'When did you last listen to the sound of chalk being grated?'

'Well, you know what I mean. What's this like?' I asked, holding up the novel in Max's line of vision.

'It's good,' said Max, pausing as he reached the top of a scale. 'About the search for the killer of a teenage girl with spots. A talented but tortured violinist is the prime suspect. They've already found the murder weapon – a sharpened bow.'

'Oh, ha, ha, very funny.'

He finished the scale. 'So go away if you don't like me playing.'

'You can hear it all over the house.'

'You can't hear it all over the house.'

'And anyway, I'm bored.'

But I wasn't bored. I was frightened.

'What if she never comes back?' I asked Max, putting the book down.

He propped his violin up against the wall and sat down next to me on the bed.

'Of course she'll come back. Why wouldn't she?'

'Why *would* she?'

'Because of us.'

'Maybe we're not enough.'

'Enough for what?'

'Enough to make her want to come back.'

135

'Of course we are. She came back last time. And the time before. And the time before that.'

My mother disappeared for the first time when I was nearly fourteen. At least, for the first time since her sudden disappearance eight years before. One day, we came home from school to find that she had packed a small bag, and was sitting with it by her feet in the kitchen, waiting for us.

'Where are you going?' I asked, eyeing the bag.

'Just away for a while.'

'But where?' asked Max.

'I don't know yet.'

'When will you be back?' I insisted, my voice shaking.

'I don't know that yet either.'

'But you will *be* back?'

'I'll be back.'

'What about Dad?' I asked.

'What about him?'

'Does he know you're going?'

'You can tell him if you like. Or don't if you don't want to. I really don't mind.'

'You can't just go.'

'I'm afraid I can. I should have done it years ago.'

'But what about us?' I said, beginning to cry.

'You'll be fine,' my mother said, kissing me on the cheek. 'There's absolutely nothing to cry about. There's food in the freezer, Mrs Woodley will be in to clean as usual on Wednesday, and it's not as though you haven't got a father.'

Then she kissed Max and left.

There was no point checking to see if she'd taken her passport with her. It was a running joke between Max and me that she never went anywhere without it. We used to ask her why she always kept it in her handbag when she rarely went further than London, or wherever it was that she'd started going off to for a couple of hours every fortnight, but I don't remember her ever giving us an answer.

It was quite a while before my father realised my mother had gone, that first time. If he wondered why there was no supper waiting for him, he didn't say anything. He just helped himself to a couple of gherkins from a jar, fishing them out very efficiently with his long, thin fingers, and went back into his study. At about nine o'clock, he came up to my room, swaying very slightly. 'Any sign of your mother?'

'She's gone away.'

'Where to?'

'She didn't say.'

My father raised his eyebrows.

'No, really, she didn't say,' I said quickly, worried that he would think Max and I knew something that he didn't and were somehow party to her plan, whatever it was.

'Did she say when she'd be back?'

'No. But she did say she *would* be back.'

'*Did* she?' he said, wearily.

'I'm sure she won't be gone long,' I said, feeling that it was my duty to make the best of what felt like a pretty disastrous situation. 'She only took a very small bag.'

I think she was gone for a couple of weeks that first time. We ate our way through the meals she'd left in the freezer for us. When they were finished, Max or my father put together strange but not unpleasant meals from whatever I bought at the little Spar on my way home from school. None of us mentioned our mother during those meals, but it felt as if we were all sitting there waiting for something to happen – for a phone call, or the sound of her keys in the door.

'Where did you go,' I asked tentatively when she finally returned.

'Oh, nowhere very much,' she said. And that was that. Until the next time.

'One day she won't come back,' I said to Max as he picked up his violin again and started playing a Bach partita. 'Why don't you care?'

'Of course I care. I care terribly.'

'Well, you don't look as though you do,' I said angrily.

Max stopped playing again and rolled his eyes. 'Can you really imagine Mum going off for good and never seeing us again? It isn't us she's getting away from.'

'So why don't they just get divorced?'

'She'd never do that. She doesn't believe in divorce.'

'How do you know? Have you ever asked her?'

'No.'

'Well, then.'

'But I'm sure she doesn't. She once said, *If you marry, you marry for life, whatever that life may be like.*'

'I know Dad thinks we're lying about not knowing where she is.'

'Well, we're not.'

'But he doesn't know that. It must *feel* to him like we're lying.'

'You can't know what he feels.'

'What do you think he tells Clara?'

'God knows! I'd love to hear the tale he spins! Want a game of Monopoly?'

'OK. Anything to stop you playing that horrible thing.'

If I had drawn a heart with an arrow through it at that time, I think it would probably have said 'Julia' at one end and 'Tony' at the other, with a couple of crossed out names underneath it. 'Tim'. And 'Chris', I think.

In all the months we were 'going out', I made sure Tony Wealden never met my parents.

'What's wrong with them?' he asked. 'They can't be worse than mine.'

'Nothing,' I said. Nothing, I thought, apart from the fact that my dad would probably be drunk and say something really embarrassing about me in front of you and my mum would probably not say anything at all or just not be there.

Sometimes, when we got fed up with wandering up and down the dreary High Street with its endless shoe shops, lighting showrooms and bakers, or got too cold lying in a secluded corner of the park with our hands up each other's jumpers or down each other's waistbands, he'd persuade me to go to his house, in the hope that his parents would be out. They never were. So we'd sit in the sitting room, well away from each other, trying to cover up the grass stains on our clothes and bruises on our necks, sipping Nescafé and eating digestive biscuits, while his parents looked at us with politely disapproving expressions.

'How's O-level revision going, then, Julia?' Tony's father would ask.

'Fine, thank you, Mr Wealden.'

'Wish I could say the same for Anthony. When was the last time you opened a textbook, son? You'll never pass physics at this rate. Never make anything of yourself.'

I was impressed that Mr Wealden knew his son was taking physics. I wasn't sure my father even knew that I was taking O-levels.

'Would anyone like a sausage roll?' Mrs Wealden chirped up one time, possibly to divert Mr Wealden from his animated, but not particularly interesting, lecture on the relative merits of a polytechnic or a university education. Then she made a little squeaking noise and covered her mouth with her hand. She had beautifully manicured fingernails, I noticed. And rather flushed cheeks.

'Oh, silly old me! Of course you wouldn't want pork, Julia.'

'Actually I'm not a vegetarian any more, Mrs Wealden. I stopped being one last Christmas,' I told her. 'I'd love one. Thanks.'

The one advantage of my mother's absences was the increased opportunity for Tony and me to indulge in undisturbed, unbridled foreplay. Once my father had shut himself in his study for the evening, I'd bring Tony in through the back door and up to my bedroom where, to the sound of Max's arpeggios, we'd snog for hours, our lips chapped and swollen, my cheeks rubbed raw by Tony's emerging stubble, the flies of his shiny black school trousers stretched to bursting point.

# XI

The day the Americans arrived, they closed the teacher training college. We were in the middle of lunch and the principal came in and said, 'I am sorry to have to announce that, with immediate effect – 12.15pm today, the 4th of April – I am declaring this college closed. I have just received news that the Americans are advancing on us. All of you will be safe if you keep calm and stay here until we know more about what is happening. Neither I nor my deputy, Frau Friedrich, are members of the Party. There is no reason to suppose the Americans will do any of us any harm.' And I stood up and one of the teachers said, 'Where are you going?' and I said, 'I'm going back to Berlin – I want to die for my country.' She's probably still laughing.

*Why do you say that?*

It wasn't really my country because they didn't consider me a proper German, but there I was – going to die for my country. I never questioned my decision for a moment. I never even went to my room to collect my things. I just left. And there at the crossroads was a huge black man in a uniform with a gun in his hand; I'd never seen anyone like him in real life before. And he shouted out in English, 'Hey, you, kid! You OK?' But I didn't stop. I ran into the forest and started walking. I got to a road and an army car stopped and picked me up and we passed all the tanks, which were running out of petrol so they just poured the last of the petrol over the tanks and put a match to them. There were all these burning tanks everywhere with soldiers setting off into the forest, taking off their jackets and walking on in their shirt-sleeves. Towards evening we turned off the road and stopped deep in the forest. The officer set up his radio and listened. One of the other soldiers divided the remaining rations between us. Then, one by one, the three other soldiers climbed out of the car and disappeared into the trees. The captain saw them leave but didn't try to stop them. And he said, 'Look, I'm going to have to go back and pick up more soldiers. It seems the Americans have crossed the Rhine. Some idiot failed to blow up the bridge. The American tanks are on their way. Here – take the rest of my food. You're on your own now. If you can get to Halle, I think there are still some trains to Berlin. Just keep off the main roads and you'll be fine.' And that was that. So I started to walk.

(SILENCE)

*Go on.*

And one day, very early in the morning, it was barely light – dawn must have just broken – through the trees stumbled a skeleton. I thought I must be dreaming as I walked. I hadn't slept for two days. And I just stopped and hid behind a tree and looked at this creature with its shaven head and sunken eyes. Of course it wasn't a skeleton – not quite. There was some flesh pulled tight on its face – here – and here. And spidery fingers hanging from the sleeves of a tattered striped shirt. If you had seen the image in a horror film you would have laughed – it was just too grotesque to be real. Then another skeleton appeared and then another. Each as wasted as the one before. Each staring ahead as they staggered on through the trees. Twenty, thirty, forty passed where I was hiding. I lost count. And I saw that they were being driven on by a small group of uniformed guards. Then I saw that the prisoner at the end of the line had stopped walking. And the guard nearest to him screamed out, 'You there! At the end. Keep going!' And I watched as the prisoner looked up at the sky – it was as though he was trying to warm his face in the early morning sun. But the rays were still too weak. Then, very slowly, he sank to his knees. The guard shouted, 'Get up! Keep going!' and he pushed at the prisoner's head with the barrel of his gun. And I covered my ears to muffle the sound of the bullet. But there was no bullet. The man just toppled sideways. And I saw the guard bend down and put his hand on the man's neck. Then he stood up and he brushed the pine needles from his trousers. I saw him pause for a second or two and then he rolled the body off the path, covered it with some fallen branches, and strode off through the forest to catch up with the others. And I didn't know where the prisoners were from, or what they'd done, or where the guards were taking them or why they were all so terribly thin. It was 1945 and I still didn't know that less than a mile away was a concentration camp, and I still didn't know it was called Buchenwald, and I still didn't know they were Jews. It was only later, when I saw the same pictures in newspapers and newsreels, that I thought, my God, I've seen them before. (SILENCE) And that is something that you never forget.

*Have you told this story before?*

What do you mean?

*Have you told it before?*

Who do you think I could tell it to? The neighbours in the Close?

*It's just, it sounded like a story you'd told before. Many times.*

In my head. That's where I tell it. Over and over and over. In my head.

# Chapter Twelve

I look over at the built-in cupboard in which Max used to sleep when he was a little boy and I suddenly feel terribly sad. I don't know why. It wasn't as though he used to huddle in there to escape the blows of our parents – neither of them ever hit us. Not once. Or to hide from his sister. I could be pretty vicious sometimes, but I was never *that* bad. By the time my mother started to disappear, he was too big to sleep in his cupboard. Maybe that's what all those scales and arpeggios were about.

When Max was nearly eighteen, the music stopped. One day he shut his violin in its case and I never saw it again. He told me he'd sold it.

'So where's the money?' I asked disbelievingly.

'I gave it to charity.'

'What did you do that for?'

'It seemed the right thing to do with it.'

'Getting rid of the ghastly instrument was right, but you could have kept the money.'

'Well, it's gone.'

'Where's it gone?'

'I put it in that collecting box outside W.H. Smith's. The one with the sad girl in a calliper.'

'*You're* the spastic!' I shouted. 'Mum'll go mad.'

But my mother didn't say anything very much when Max told her about the violin and the money. She was much less reticent when he explained, very calmly, that he'd given up everything else as well – like turning up for school and revising for his A-levels.

I heard them arguing as I sat in my room trying to commit swathes of *Antony and Cleopatra* and Laurie Lee to memory for my O-level English mock. 'You don't have to be a doctor,' my mother shouted over the unfamiliar sound of Pink Floyd – at least he'd started to listen to decent music rather than all that Vivaldi and Bach and other square rubbish. 'You don't have to be like any of that lot,' my mother went on. 'You don't have to get the best results in the school. You don't have to be a famous anything. Not a famous doctor, not a famous violinist. Whoever said you did?'

'No one had to say it.'

'You just have to stay at school and take your A-levels.'

'What's the point?'

'Why throw it all away now?'

'I'm not throwing anything away.'

'You are. It's your education. Do your A-levels and then you can do anything you like.'

'Like what?'

'Like get a degree. Have a career.'

'And what's the point of that? *You* never got a degree.'

'And don't you think I wish I had?' she raged. 'Don't you think I'd like to have done a degree when I was your age, if things had been different, instead of struggling away trying to study now? Don't you think it would be nice if your grandmother hadn't been able to look down her nose at me all these years?'

'She doesn't look down her nose at you.'

'Oh, no? Generations of physicists and doctors and surgeons marrying professors of maths and professional musicians and lawyers. And then her son, the famous doctor, marries some nobody who just had children and a nervous breakdown and never did anything else again. You think she didn't laugh? Don't be ridiculous. They all did.'

'Dad wasn't famous when he married you. And he never laughed at anything you did.'

'He never noticed what I did. Do you think he knows what I'm doing now? Do you think he ever wonders where I go every day?'

'But if you told him, he'd probably be quite interested.'

'Max. Just do as I ask and stay at school. You've got less than two terms left. If you leave now, you won't hurt your father or your grandmother or any of the rest of them. You'll only hurt yourself. Do you think your father would even notice?'

'I'm not trying to hurt anyone. Why would I want to do that?'

'No? Well, just think about it.'

'I've thought about it, Mum. I haven't thought about anything else for weeks.'

'Please, Max. Do it for me. If you won't do it for yourself.'

I wonder what my grandmother would have said to someone trying to fit Max into her family tree? *And then there was Max – but don't bother to write him down.* But I'm being unfair. She continued to enjoy his visits, long after he left home to eventually study art in Leeds after working in a hostel for homeless men for a couple of years. I imagine her shaking her head sadly over their game of chess and saying, *Your great-grandfather was a famous doctor, your grandfather was a famous doctor, your father was a famous doctor and you, too, could have been a famous doctor.* And I imagine Max just smiling at her kindly, moving his knight across the board to safety.

'Why *did* you give it all up, Max?' I asked him one time when I went up to Leeds to see him.

'All what?'

'All your music. All your being brilliant at everything.'

'I wasn't brilliant at everything.'

'You were.'

'Only in comparison with you.'

'Shut up!'

'You asked for it.'

'But, seriously, what happened that day? When you gave up the violin and everything?'

'Nothing happened on a particular day. And I didn't give up everything. I gave in, you might remember. I stayed at school. I got those A-levels Mum cared so much about.'

'But people don't change overnight for no reason. Something must have happened to you. People don't just suddenly give everything up.'

'What did I give up?'

'The chance to be as unhappy as Dad, maybe? Was that what all that was about?'

'It's not that simple.'

'But that must've had something to do with it. What good did it ever do him – being the best? Being famous? Who remembers him now?'

I saw Max swallow.

'We do.'

'But that's not what he cared about. He just wanted his mother to be proud of him.'

'She was. She was always going on about how incredibly famous he was.'

'But she stopped, didn't she? When he started to shake too much to operate. When they suggested he might like to take some leave and perhaps not try to rush back to work too soon.'

'He was hugely respected at the hospital. Didn't you used to tell me how much the nurses loved him?'

'Yeah, well. Let's not go there.'

'Okay, perhaps not.'

'You know, it took them less than a week to paint over his name in the hospital car park. I went to have a look. Some

147

ambitious registrar must have opened a bottle of champagne the day they announced Dad's death. All that work, all the time he didn't spend with us – what was it all for?'

'There are lots of parents out there who remember Dad, I'm sure, and lots of children who are alive today because of him,' said Max, and I could see that his eyes were brimming with tears.

'Do you think they even knew he had children of his own?'

'I don't know. I doubt it. Why?'

'I sometimes wonder if we existed for him at all, the moment he drove out of the Close. I mind, you know.'

'Mind what?'

'That Dad was only ever really happy when he was at work. When we weren't around. It was never *us* who made him happy.'

'We don't know that. There's nothing much we *do* know about him so I don't think we can hazard a guess at what, if anything, made him happy.'

'But what about you, Max? Are you happy now?'

'What do you think?' He smiled at me and suddenly everything began to feel a bit better.

I looked round his tiny studio room, at the dirty skylight, the jars of brushes on the floor, the half-finished canvases piled up against the wall, the unmade bed. 'It's hard to tell, really.'

'Well, I am, actually. Very. Though I miss the men at the hostel. They still write, one or two of them, which is nice. But the other students in this house are really great. We cook together and stuff. And you? Is all your exotic travelling making you happy? Thanks for that thing, by the way,' he said, nodding up at the wall from where a dark wooden mask with tufts of reddish-brown hair glared out at us.

'I thought it would remind you of me.' I laughed.

'Not quite angry enough. Or ugly enough.'

'Shut up! And it's not just exotic travelling. It's part of my course. And I'm thinking of going back to West Africa when I graduate. There's an incredible anthropologist I want to work with.'

'Oh, yes?' Max looked at me quizzically, a smile playing round his eyes.

'What?' I said, and realised too late how defensive I sounded.

'Nothing. It's just the way you looked when you said *incredible*. Like this.'

Max put on a dreamy, lovestruck expression. I picked up a pillow from his bed and hurled it at him. It caught one of the jars of brushes. A stream of turpentine flowed towards the wall. Max untied his scarf and blotted the liquid up just before it reached the canvases.

'Sorry,' I said.

He smiled.

'No problem.'

# XII

It took me over two weeks to get to Berlin. I got there on the 20th of April. I stood on Alexanderplatz and suddenly there were bombs dropping. And I looked up and I couldn't see any planes. There was a man standing next to me and he pulled me back and said, 'The Russians are shelling Berlin!' And I thought, you stupid idiot! The Russians are nowhere near Berlin – we're winning this war. I got home and my father was there, sitting in his summer house and he looked a bit surprised to see me and he just said, 'What are you doing here? Have a bath and wash your clothes – you stink.' And I said to him, 'People are saying the Russians are coming. What are you going to do?' And he said, 'I think I'll go out for lunch.' So I had a bath and changed into the SS man's woollen trousers, an old pullover and a jacket, which was all I could find in my wardrobe. And I took my wooden angel from under the floorboard where I'd hidden her. And a little red leather notebook that Effie Feldt had given me for my last birthday. And I put them in one pocket and my identity card in my other. And then as I was towelling my hair dry, I looked out of the window and I saw that the tanks were coming up our road. I went out of the back door and I ran. And I met my mother who was coming back from the shops – she had some sugar and some oats and some apples – and before she could even greet me or ask me what I was doing back in Berlin I said, 'Run! There are Russian tanks coming up our road!'

(SILENCE)

*What did you do?*

We ran for about a mile until we came to a factory and the door was open. It was teeming with people, all moving towards the cellar. I recognised a Swiss family from our street but, apart from them, the rest of the crowd seemed to be factory workers – mostly Poles. For three days, my mother and I and about two hundred other people stayed crammed in that cellar while bombs were exploding all around us. So much for us winning the war. So much for the Russians having been forced back at the border. It was so crowded that we had to take it in turns to sit down. By the second day, everyone's food had been shared out and there was nothing left. The smell of urine and faeces is something I'll never forget. On the third day, the bombing stopped. We thought everything was over – that we'd be all right. Then suddenly the door burst open and we were all ordered out. The Russian soldiers didn't seem to notice the stench that greeted them. They shouted at us in Russian – trying to separate the Poles and the Germans into two groups. The Swiss family were trying to make them understand that they were neither German nor Polish and should be allowed to go free. A fight broke out – I don't know what about – and for a second or two nobody was guarding the door. I grabbed my mother's hand and we just ran.

*And then what happened?*

We just ran and walked. From the 22nd of April until the 31st of May.

(SILENCE)

*Go on.*

We walked at night. We ate when we found food. One time we came across a burnt-out farmhouse and a group of men and women and a few children, all as thin and filthy as we were, were sitting in the cellar. It was piled high with glass jars of gherkins, cabbage and celeriac, piles of dried sausage and smoked ham. And we sat and ate until we thought we would burst. Then one of the men patted his swollen stomach, picked up an unfinished jar of beetroot and threw it against the wall. It looked as if there'd been a massacre! And then all the others picked up jars and smashed them – even my mother, who never wasted a thing. If we couldn't finish the food, and we couldn't take it with us, no Russian was going to get any.

# *Chapter Thirteen*

It's impossible not to hear the sound of the violin in this room. It's as though the walls have absorbed the millions of notes that have been played here. I find it hard to believe that, in the silences between the bursts of computer-generated automatic rifle fire, the sharp detonation of caps, and the sound of wailing boy bands, Ben and his sisters don't sometimes hear the distant sound of Bach or Vivaldi.

'Don't you miss it?' I asked Max on one of my visits back to England, when he had been living and working in a sheltered community in Devon for a few years. We were lying side by side on his ancient bed in one of the huge old shared houses, as the only chair in the room was doubling up as his wardrobe and filing cabinet.

'Miss what?'

'Your hideous violin.'

'You obviously don't.'

'I don't miss the endless practising – the same two bars played a thousand times.'

'Do you think you might be exaggerating just a little bit?'

'Who, *me*?'

Max smiled. Rather sadly, I thought.

'I tried to buy it back, you know,' he said. 'I was going to borrow the money from Clara.'

'So why didn't you?'

'It was gone by the time I got back to the shop. It was quite a rare instrument. Someone would have been pleased to get their hands on it.'

'Couldn't you have found out who had bought it and asked them to sell it back to you?'

'I suppose so, but I thought maybe it was a sign.'

'What kind of sign?'

'A reminder of the consequences of decisions made in haste.'

'You're mental.'

'So you've so often said. And I thought we'd been through all this. Years ago.'

'You could have got it back easily if you'd tried. You were really good. You could have been a professional musician. Don't you ever wonder what would have happened if you'd not sold it? Or if you'd borrowed the money and bought another violin? It didn't have to be the one Mum gave you. You might not have had to live in a hostel in Islington, or a shit-hole in Leeds for years. Or live in this Munster House now with a bunch of spastics.'

'I loved the hostel and the Leeds place was quite cosy, actually, and this "Munster House" is a brilliant place to live. And, just for your information, people with cerebral palsy aren't called spastics any more.'

'I do know that,' I said, ashamed as usual.

'I know you do,' he said kindly. 'And anyway, what's the point of looking back all the time – wondering how things might have been, what would have happened if things had been different? Things are just how they are or how they were.'

'What's the point in *not* wondering?'

'So you can get on with your life.'

'Is that what you are doing?'

'I suppose it is. What I'm trying to do, anyway.'

'And you're saying I'm not?'

'I didn't say that at all.'

'But you thought it.'

'I didn't, actually.'

'You make me feel like some kind of freak,' I shouted.

'It's your new hairdo and the tan.'

'Don't laugh at me.'

'Well, don't be so daft, then. How can I possibly make you feel like a freak?'

'The way you just accept everything that happens to you. That happened to you when you were a child. The way you just see the good in everything. It makes me *sick*!'

'I don't think I see the good in everything. I try to – but it doesn't always work. Some things that happen make it really hard.'

He stopped and turned his face away from mine. Each time we met, it was our father's death to which our meandering conversations returned. And each time we talked about him, Max's eyes would fill with tears and mine would stay resolutely dry, while I felt a knot tighten in my throat until I thought I'd suffocate.

'It was good Dad died so suddenly,' I said after a while, when I felt it was safe to try to breathe again. 'And without any pain or anything. He'd have made a crap hospital patient.'

'You'll have to watch it. You're starting to see the good in everything,' said Max, wiping his face with the corner of the frayed cotton bedspread.

'But don't you ever wonder who that woman was, at his funeral?' I couldn't help asking.

'Which woman?'

'The youngish one with long curly brown hair, standing a bit apart when everyone was leaving the crematorium.'

'I don't remember any young woman with long curly brown hair.'

'You must do. I pointed her out to you.'

'Given that we know absolutely nothing about Dad's life apart from what Clara used to tell us, it could have been anyone. His secretary, a grown-up patient, a junior doctor, a nurse, the person from the off-licence where he bought his whisky and fags.'

'But who do you think it was?'

'I don't know.'

'But don't you want to know?'

'Why would I want to know?'

'I don't know. To make sense of things.'

'How would knowing who that woman was make sense of anything? It's as though you're always hoping that something will suddenly drop into place. People aren't jigsaws. You can't just look for missing pieces to slot in and complete the picture. Life's not some kind of puzzle that you have to solve before you can get on with your own.'

'What if she was his secret love-child? Wouldn't that make you feel different about knowing or not knowing?'

'It might, I suppose, though I've always found having *one* sister quite a challenge.'

I went up to the window. A couple of magpies were strutting about on the flat roof. Two for joy. I wondered if my father ever felt joy. I wondered again what he felt when his hands began to shake too much to allow him to hold a scalpel, when there were no more press cuttings and publications for his mother to paste into her scrapbooks, when there was nothing left of him for her to be proud of. I wondered what he was thinking in the moments before he shut his eyes and his heart stopped and the cigarette fell out of his mouth.

I went with Max to the hospital mortuary where my father's body had been taken. Max went in first. I sat on a red plastic sofa in the little anteroom watching a nurse making notes in a cardboard file at a desk in the corner. From time to time she looked up and smiled at me kindly. There was a little hole in the sofa from which a small clump of white nylon stuffing billowed. I forced it back in and pressed the pieces of torn red plastic together. Then Max came out and sat down next to me. I felt my fingers creeping towards his leg. He took my hand and squeezed it. For a moment I thought we were back in Miss Everett's class and that everything would be all right. I could feel his body shake as he sat there, crying quietly.

'It's your turn,' he said after a while, letting go of my hand and wiping the tears from his face with the back of his hand.

'I don't think I can go in.'

'It was OK, actually.'

'I don't want to see him dead.'

'I think you'll regret it if you don't. It's important that you see him. Go on. I'll wait for you here.'

I draw up a chair to the bed on which my father has been laid out. He doesn't look dead, just different. I put my hand on his, feeling his long, thin fingers. I can't remember the last time I touched him. I can't remember what I said to him the last time I saw him. I hope it was something kind but I'm not sure that it was. I want to say something to him now, even though it's too late. Something important. I want to say, *I told you this would happen, but you never listened.* I want to say, *I need you to know that I loved you all those times I shouted and threw my books around your study.* I want to say, *I loved our silent journeys. I loved the crazy meals you made us.* I want to say, *I wish I'd known you.*

I kiss him on his cold forehead.

'Bye, Dad,' I say.

We thought my grandmother would give up and die when her only child – her genius son – predeceased her. At his funeral she looked like a tiny, frail old woodland creature, her rheumy eyes staring at the floor, her gnarled hands clutching the pew in the crematorium chapel. But when Max and I visited her a few weeks later it was as though she'd never had a son. Over coffee and plum cake, she talked about the lamentable decline in available bridge partners; about the new cash registers at the supermarket which none of the stupid girls had learned to operate properly. She asked Max if it was now time to stop all that nonsense work with the down-and-outs and take up his place at art school; or, better still, apply to a proper university. Perhaps it was not too late to do medicine after all. She told me she wasn't surprised that I hadn't had the intellectual ability to get into Oxford, but that I'd probably enjoy Edinburgh once I'd learned to understand the horrible accent. *And what is this anthropology? Is it really a serious subject to study at university? It is such shame you are too unintelligent to study medicine. To be a doctor.* Of my father there was no mention. *And then there was Clara Eisenstein who married Arthur Rosenthal 1925, and they had, in 1926, Oscar – no don't bother to write him down.*

My grandmother was very keen to reach a hundred. She didn't care about the telegram from the Queen – *for in Germany I am already so very famous.* In her centenary year, she appeared in a well-received German television documentary about the lives of German exiles between 1935 and 1950. She was awarded some kind of honorary chair at a new medical school in Hamburg. And then, having reached her target during an extended trip to Germany, she came back to Oxford to die. Unfortunately for her, all those decades of swimming and fruit-picking worked against her. Her body refused to obey. Finally, at a hundred and four, she put her papers in order, locked up her house, admitted herself into an upmarket nursing home and, very efficiently, starved herself to death.

The magpies on the roof were ousted by a group of starlings squabbling over a piece of mouldy bread. I heard the mattress squeak as Max got off his bed and came up behind me. He wrapped his arms around me.

'You'll be fine. We'll both be fine. The sins of the fathers, if there really were any sins, don't have to be carried down the generations. We can make our own futures. Our own kinds of families in any way we choose. Like I've chosen these people here as my family. Hey! You're finally getting fat! I hadn't noticed before. It must be all that rice and groundnut stew you've been eating.'

I waited for a few seconds – a few seconds in which Max's hands tightened round my waist and I felt his warm breath on my neck.

'God! Julia. How pregnant *are* you?' he said very quietly.

'Nearly five months,' I replied, keeping my eyes on the starlings.

Max went back to his bed and sat down.

'Was that part of the plan?' he asked.

'I was the one who alphabetised my books, remember? And did fantastically complicated revision timetables. I was school librarian. I loved filing. I'm not exactly the *having an accident* kind of person. If I were, this would be a little Tony Wealden or some other St Peter's reject.'

'But you were always pretty crap at maths. And you didn't think Tony Wealden was a reject at the time. Quite the opposite, I always thought, judging by the terrible noises the two of you made. You used to put me off my violin practice.'

'You can't possibly have heard us from two rooms away. And this wasn't an accident,' I said, lying down beside him and putting my hands over my small bulge.

'So who's the father?'

'Well, that's the slightly complicated bit. Well, not really *slightly* complicated.'

'Don't tell me. The incredible anthropologist.'

'How did you know that?'

'You're a lot more obvious than you'd like to think. What's he like?'

'Lovely. And old.'

'Like really old or just a bit older than you?'

'Really old. Nearly sixty.'

'God, Julia! Is this Oedipal or what?'

'And married. With children.'

'Oh, great!'

'About my age – the children are.'

'Isn't this taking your anthropological research into the family and kinship a little too far?'

'Since when have you been the expert on relationships? With your string of weeping, abandoned women and crazy made-up families of society's misfits and cripples.'

'I've never abandoned anyone. I've just never wanted that kind of relationship: just me and one other person living in a little house together. I've always been very clear about that, whoever I've been with. And we're all misfits and cripples in some way, don't you think?'

'Speak for yourself.'

'Is the baby going to know its father?'

'I hope so. But it's tricky.'

'Does his wife know?'

'No. And she isn't going to.'

'How do you feel about that?'

'Bad. About the lie.'

'More a lack of truth.'

'I suppose so. Is that better or worse?'

'Don't ask me – Mum was always the one with the complex theory of truth and lies. Does she know about the baby?'

'Not yet. She's in transit again, I think. I'll tell her when she next sends me her address.'

'What do you think she'll say?'

'I've no idea.'

'Nor me. So it'll just be you and the baby?'

'That's the idea.'

'It'll be very hard. Have you really thought about it?'

'Look, it's not exactly as though our father played a huge part in our childhood. And at least my baby won't grow up being torn in two all the time. Maybe a father who really isn't there is better than a father who is there, but isn't. And maybe a happy single mother is better than an unhappy married one. At least I'll have the chance to do it right.'

'Mum and Dad didn't do that badly.'

'I didn't say they did. But there are lots of things I'll do differently. And some things I'll make bloody sure I do better.'

'So what's his name? The very old anthropologist?'

'I can't tell you.'

'Don't be daft.'

'I can't. I promised I'd never tell anyone.'

'He can't make you do that.'

'It was my idea, not his.'

'Why would you want to live with a secret like that hanging over you?'

'If it's really only me who knows who the father is, then nothing bad can come of it. No one need ever be hurt.'

'How did you work that one out?'

'Look, it makes sense to me, and that's what matters, isn't it?'

'What about this one?' Max asked, pointing at my stomach.

'What about it?'

'What'll you tell the baby?'

'I don't know. I'll work something out.'

'Clara will be pleased that the family name will live on. I'm assuming you won't be giving the baby its father's surname?'

'No. And not mine, either.'

'What are you going to do? Just make up a name?'

'I am, actually.'

'Well, that's different.'

'It'll be fine.'

'Leave Cameroon, Julia. Come back and live here with me. In my lovely Munster House.'

'I can't. I've got a career and a life to get on with.'

'What if the baby-with-the-made-up-surname gets some terrible tropical disease?'

'Millions of babies grow up perfectly healthily in Africa.'

'And millions don't. Live here with me. I'd look after you both.'

'I know you would. And it's good to know that.'

Max rested his head on my stomach.

'Does it move at all?'

'Lots. Especially in the evening. And if I'm listening to music. Sod's law it'll be musically talented. You can be bloody sure I'll never let it anywhere near a violin!'

'Hello, baby,' Max whispered to the little bump. 'You're going to need all the help you can get with my crazy sister for a mother. But I'll be here for you.'

I took a handful of Max's blond curls and pulled. Very hard.

# XIII

*Go on.*

I told you. We just ran and walked. From the 22nd of April until the 31st of May.

(SILENCE)

*Do you want to tell me any more?*

I really can't.

*You really can't remember?*

Can't remember? I can't forget.

*So tell me. The things you can't forget.*

And then what? Is that supposed to make me feel better?

*It might. Have you told anyone else?*

Told them what?

*What you did? What you saw? All those things that you can't forget?*

You keep asking me that. Who should I tell? The postman? The man who reads the electricity meter? Who do I ever see? Who could I possibly tell?

*You've never spoken about this to anyone?*

Never.

*You must have told someone.*

No one.

*You have never told anyone any of the things you have told me over the past few months?*

I tell the ghosts. In my head. Over and over and over. They go round and round, year after year – the stories in my head. Over and over and over. Sometimes they change a bit. But not much.

*Try and tell me. Think of me as one of those ghosts.*

(LONG SILENCE)

We travelled by night, sleeping by day in forests, ditches or burned-out farms. It was unusually warm, the spring of 1945, but the nights were still cold and we'd wake up with numb fingers and blue lips. Every time we stopped to sleep, I'd get out my little red leather notebook and record the date and the name of the nearest town or village if I knew it. I don't know why. It seemed important at the time. Often we came across young German soldiers wanting to know whether the war had ended yet, where the Russians or Americans were, and whether we had any food. On April the 25th we met up with a small group of factory workers and travelled with them for a few days. They were an optimistic crowd, convinced that it wouldn't be long until the war would be over and there would be an end to all the running. On the third night of travelling together, we'd walked about half a kilometre along a little dirt track when I realised I'd left my notebook in the hollow tree trunk I'd been resting in during the day. I told my mother to go on with the factory crowd and I'd catch them up. I remember it was a full moon and it didn't take me long to retrace my steps to the tree and there was my notebook where I'd left it. So I stuffed it deep into the pocket of my black trousers with my angel and my identity card. And then I heard this voice – '*Hey!*

*Germanski!'* And I turned round and there was this Russian soldier. I can still see his face so clearly. Those dark slanting eyes. He grinned at me. His teeth were chipped and tobacco-stained. He took my arm and I jerked it free. He wasn't smiling any more. He grabbed my wrist and I bit him in the hand, as hard as I could. God, was he angry! I saw him pick up his gun with both hands, and he smashed the butt into my face.

(SILENCE)

*And then?*

And that's the end of that particular story.

*Is it?*

It is. So after – after some time – I carried on walking through the forest, hoping I'd find my mother and the factory workers again, but I didn't. Everywhere I walked, there were scenes of such terrible destruction. Whole villages lying empty; goats and cows with bullet holes through their heads, crawling with maggots and bluebottles; a woman lying dead outside her burning house, her dress around her head. All those bruises and the blood – blood everywhere. Have you ever smelt congealing blood? And then one day the Russians found a group of us searching for food in an abandoned farm and they took us away. They marched us to the edge of a lake where they arranged us into a line along a wooden landing stage. There were eight or nine of us. Men and women and one small boy who was clinging to his mother's leg and crying. The girl next to me was about my age. We'd become quite good friends over the past few days of scavenging together. And they aimed a machine gun at us. And they pointed to the first man and said, *'Germanski?'* And he said, *'Ruski.'* And they laughed. And shot him. And then they pointed at the mother with her child and said, *'Germanski?'* And she just shook her head and clutched her child, too terrified to

165

say anything. And they shot them both. And then they said the same to me and I said, '*Hollandski,*' and shut my eyes. And they said, '*Hollandski! Komm!*' And, as they drove me towards their camp in a nearby farmhouse, I could hear the crackle of the machine gun and the splashes as, one by one, the bodies fell into the lake. (LONG SILENCE) I still remember that girl's name. The one who stood next to me. Christiana. I can still see her standing there next to me. Even now, when I shut my eyes.

(LONG SILENCE)

*Go on. If you can.*

They took me to a Russian officer who spoke some Dutch. And it's amazing how, with a gun at your head, you can suddenly become fluent in a language you've barely spoken a word of for thirteen years. The officer was keen to show off his Dutch. He opened a drawer full of watches. 'Look! You want one? Just choose. Look at mine.' And as his jacket rode up, like this, I could see five or six watches on each arm. It was chaos outside – soldiers were chasing pigs round the yard. There was all this squealing and shouting. Then there were gunshots and then silence. And then the officer asked me if I could cook. I'd have to do it outside as the stove in the kitchen was broken. And so a young soldier butchered the warm pigs and I cooked the pork on a fire in a field behind the farmhouse while the officers sat inside drinking vodka. And very carefully with a knife I made a hole in the pocket of my SS man's trousers, and very carefully I slid my identity card down the inside of my trousers to my shoe and into the fire. It curled and went black and then was gone.

*And then?*

And then he let me go, the Russian with the watches. There was nothing left for me to cook and they were moving on.

He was sorry I didn't want to take a watch. He shook his head very sadly as I turned to go. They weren't all as decent as he was.

(LONG SILENCE)

Somewhere in a forest near a hollow tree are quite a few of my teeth.

*Your teeth?*

Maybe somewhere in Mongolia there's an old man with a faint bite mark on his hand and a vague memory of a very thin, half-naked girl running into the forest with her black woollen trousers in her hand. Maybe he can remember blood dripping from the butt of his rifle. I'd like to think he remembers.

(LONG SILENCE)

*And what happened next?*

On the 31st of May, I walked into a Red Cross camp. 'You know the war ended on May the 8th,' a Red Cross nurse told me as she took off all my clothes – my SS man's trousers, my pullover and jacket – and burned them. Then she cut off all my hair to get rid of the lice and washed me in disinfectant. And she put some antiseptic on my infected, bleeding gums. I stood there in a towel holding the only things in the world that I owned – a little wooden angel and a red leather notebook. The nurse gave me some underwear and a cotton dress. I remember it had blue and pink flowers on it. She asked me where I'd come from, and when I said Berlin, and that I'd been walking for six weeks, trying to get to Holland, she told me she'd deloused another Dutch woman a few days ago who'd said the same thing and who was probably still somewhere in the camp. She said I'd need to talk to the Americans. I wouldn't be able to get into Holland without identity papers or a passport. But all I could think of was finding my mother.

(SILENCE)

*And did you? Find your mother?*

I didn't recognise her at first. I walked past a bald woman with fresh scars on her face and neck sitting a little way apart from the others. If she hadn't called out my name, I would never have seen my mother again. We got hold of enough papers to get us out of the camp – I can't remember how exactly. Then we managed to get a lift in the back of an army truck to the border, and so we ended up back in Holland, where we'd come from all those years ago. We walked to my grandparents' house, and rang the bell, and they came to the door together and told us to go round the back if we wanted some food. It was only when my mother spoke that they realised who we were. And how pleased they must have been to see me, my grandmother and her neighbours! The German with the missing teeth and shaven head in a borrowed dress.

*But your grandfather must have been happy to see you?*

He was. Whenever my grandmother was out of the way, he'd come and find me and take my hand and squeeze it or stroke my head.

*And you stayed there?*

Where else could we go? We had nothing. I was under house arrest for a while. Then I had to report to the police station every day. If I kept out of the way of my grandmother, life wasn't too bad.

# Chapter Fourteen

The door to Angie and Geoff's bedroom is open. I go in and look out over the green. I shut my eyes and walk out into the Close to school. Out of the front door, round to the right. At number three were the Fletchers. Tomas, a boy of about my age, Mrs Fletcher who was big, blonde and Swedish, and Mr Fletcher whom we rarely saw. Tomas used to do a lot of naughty things, often involving damage to other children's property or bodies. He'd probably have a label of some kind now. And medication, too, no doubt. 'Wait till your father gets home, Tomas!' his mother would screech out of the front door in Swedish. Or at least that's what Tomas told us she was shouting as he sat with us on the green, ignoring her, eating flying saucers and sherbet fountains. Max and I wondered if Tomas's father minded being given the job of beating his son on his return from work. What if he'd rather sit down with a drink and the newspaper than get his belt out? And, if they were going to beat him, why didn't Mrs Fletcher do it herself? She was a lot bigger than Mr Fletcher.

At number two was a family with three children. The middle child had his leg in a calliper, I remember, but I can't recall their names or anything much else about them. I don't think they played out the front very often. I remember the boy at number one – Brian Nunn – who went to Max's school and was given the task of escorting us for part of the journey when I first started school. This he did with some considerable reluctance, striding off ahead of us and occasionally pausing to check that we were still dawdling behind him, then striding off again before we could catch up and embarrass him further. When we first moved to the Close, Brian was a smartly turned-out twelve-year-old, with a neat side parting, whose shiny black shoes were always tidily lined up in his parents' glass porch. Max and I watched with interest as, over the years, Brian transformed into a Hell's Angel, albeit a fairly benign one, and the shoes were replaced by huge leather boots with silver buckles. We thought it was rather nice for Brian's parents that Hell's Angels still remembered to take their shoes off inside. We quite missed Brian when he left home. At eighteen, he was no longer embarrassed by us and used to talk us through the finer points of his Harley Davidson as he polished it on Saturday mornings – though I'm sure the rest of the residents of Tenterden Close, if not his parents, were relieved when he finally packed his panniers and roared off for the open road.

Coming home, I'd walk the other way round the Close. At number eight was the Heaney family, Mr and Mrs Heaney and four girls, each a year apart, who all went to the local convent school. Over the years, all four had a crush on Max, who tolerated their notes and gifts and invitations to come out and play with his usual good grace. At number seven were Mr and Mrs Tate, a childless couple in their fifties, who sometimes, in the summer, let us use their very small swimming pool. Mr Tate was a bit of a handyman and had built a bar out of shiny knotted pine in the corner of their sitting room. Drambuie, Martini, sherry, crème de menthe, curaçao, advocaat. I loved the colours as much as the exotic names. Sometimes we'd perch on the leather-look and chrome bar stools and Mr Tate would produce multicoloured drinks from the mixers he kept in the fridge, finishing them off with a parasol or a glacé cherry or a pale green olive on a stick. 'Bottoms up!' he'd say with a wink as he handed them over to us and downed his own rather less virgin cocktail. I thought the Tates were the most glamorous people in the world. Mr Tate had twinkly eyes and a neat little moustache. He always wore a navy blazer and cream slacks and often sported a silk cravat. Mrs Tate clacked about the house in high-heeled sandals and caftans, long fake eyelashes and shiny fake nails. They seemed to have a lot more fun than the rest of the grown-ups I came across. They were the first people in the Close to own a colour television; eventually they had to pretend to be out to stop the hordes of children ringing their bell, begging to be allowed to watch *Crackerjack* in colour.

The Feelys lived at number six. Peter and his sister Rosalind, who were our best friends in the Close. Our friendship survived my accidental assault on Peter with a rounders bat and his impressive black eye which his mother, rather inexplicably, smeared with butter. And Rosalind's patient, but ultimately unsuccessful, wooing of Max. Our next-door neighbours were the Croziers. The boys, Michael and John, were boarders somewhere in Kent so we didn't see much of them. Sometimes, during the holidays, Peter, Rosalind, Max and I would call on them to come out and play. Mrs Crozier would open the door a few inches and call into the house, 'It's the little Jews from next door.' I wasn't sure that that was very polite and even less sure that the Feelys really *were* Jewish.

I look around the room. It is as messy as the rest of the house. Angie's bedside table is piled high with clothing catalogues and women's magazines. I pick up the chunky catalogue at the top of the stack and flick through it, despising the perfect long-haired mummies with their banal aphorisms, their fitted floral skirts, their cardigans sporting 'fun buttons', their brightly coloured ballet pumps and co-ordinating, laughing, tousle-haired children. Despising the smug daddies with their moleskin trousers and jaunty shirts, their shiny white smiles, their manly grins and chiselled jaws. I want to take a thick black pen and cancel them all out. I want to add wrinkles and worry lines, and spots and tears. A weak chin or two.

I realise that I've not had anything to eat all day.

On the floor beside the bed is a pile of newspapers. And there it is. That colour supplement. Unread. About four from the top.

There is a note of caution, almost anxiety, in Susanna's voice when she rings. So different from her usual upbeat, confident tone.

'Have you read it yet, Mum?'

'Well, just the introd – ' I begin.

'It's just that when you didn't call…' she interrupts.

'I've been meaning to – '

'Some things came out a bit… not as I meant them to, really. They sound sort of critical. It's mostly just the way he edited the interview. You know what journalists are like. He wouldn't let me see it before they published it – that's the policy apparently. Even though he's a friend of George's. And I had to work really hard on Max to get him to agree to be interviewed. He wasn't at all keen at the beginning.'

I recognise the need for absolution in Susanna's voice, know that for the first time in her twenty-six years she desperately wants me to push her fair hair from her face, to see what is written on her forehead and make everything all right. It is a new feeling for her and not one with which she feels at all comfortable. I should feel pity for her, but I realise with a rush of shame that what I feel is something akin to triumph – that finally my daughter would know what it had always been like for me. What it could have been like for her if I had arranged our lives differently.

'It's great. Really interesting.'

'Are you sure?' The relief in Susanna's voice is tangible. 'There's been lots more interest in the business too, this past couple of days. So that's good, isn't it?'

'Look, Susanna. I've got to go and give a lecture now. I'm really sorry. We'll talk about this properly another time. Give my love to George.'

'OK, Mum. I'll see you soon. And thanks.'

'For what?'

'For being so good about the article. I knew you would be. It's just… I really don't want you to feel – '

'Off you go and have fun.'

'OK. Say hi to Dan from me when he gets back from India.'

I put down the phone and go not to give a lecture but back to bed, leaving the magazine unread on the floor. Would my mother count this as a white lie, or one of those bigger, more lethal ones? I wonder, as I pull the duvet over my head. I think back to that hot summer when I finally gave in and brought Susanna to England to live with Max and the rest of his 'family'. I stayed with them for a few days, trying to work out who in the big old house was related to whom, how it all worked and how anything got done. I agreed with Max that I'd leave Susanna with him for a fortnight and then come back to see how things were working out. I was desperate for it to be cold and rainy, for her to change her mind about living in England, but the sun continued to shine in a cloudless sky and there was no phone call from Susanna begging me to come and collect her. I returned a couple of days earlier than arranged and, as I walked up the garden path, I heard music coming from the back of the house. I walked round into the garden and there were Max and Susanna playing violin and flute duets. Susanna saw me first, smiling at me with her eyes. I stood and waited until they had finished, then went and put my arms round her. She buried her head in my neck and hugged me very tightly. 'I've missed you, Mum,' she said. But somehow I knew then that she wouldn't be going back with me.

'How come you never told me Max could play the violin?' Susanna asked me over dinner.

'He hasn't played since he was about seventeen. I thought you sold your violin, Max?'

'I did. I borrowed this one from the music department so I could play with Susanna. She's really good.'

'So's he, Mum. *Really* good. I always wondered how come I could possibly be musical with you as a mother.'

'And now it all makes sense,' I said.

'Absolutely.'

# XIV

The good die young, they say. My mother died in the winter of 1947. We never spoke of those weeks in the forest. I guessed what had happened to her but I couldn't ask and she never told me. We shared a room in my grandparents' house and she used to cry out in her sleep and wake up drenched in sweat. Night after night. And I'd know what she was dreaming about. I was having the same dream. There are some things you just can't talk about. *You* think it makes it better, talking about things. But there are some things you can't bear to even think about. And if you can't even think of them, how can you begin to talk about them?

*And your grandparents?*

My grandfather did his best to make me feel welcome. Unlike my grandmother, he didn't care what the neighbours thought about them harbouring an emaciated, shaven-headed German.

(LONG SILENCE)

*Are you all right?*

And then he died. About a year and a half after we moved in with them. He had become quite confused in those last months of his life, but he recognised me right up to the end. He'd lie in his bed, stroking my hand and calling me his little radish.

*Have a tissue.*

Thanks. My grandmother waited until my mother had died before she allowed herself the pleasure of informing me that my grandfather was actually no blood relative of mine.

*What do you mean?*

Just that. He wasn't really my grandfather.

*Who was he, then?*

The best friend of a Jewish lawyer who got my grandmother pregnant and then wouldn't marry her because she wasn't a Jew. He did the decent thing, my grandfather. He married my grandmother and brought up my mother as his own child.

*Do you think that was true?*

What was true?

*What your grandmother told you.*

I refused to believe it at first. I thought it was just a malicious game. To punish me.

*Punish you for what?*

For being a German. And for having the audacity to believe that someone as good and kind as my grandfather could possibly have been related to me.

*Perhaps she made it up.*

She was very organised, my grandmother. She had all the evidence filed away for me. The adoption papers. And the obituary of my real grandfather. Anton Schenck. A successful lawyer and pillar of the community who died in Florida. She sat there smiling while I read through all the evidence. And don't ask how that made me feel. I'm not going to talk about it. Not now. Maybe not ever.

*And your father? What happened to him?*

I didn't see him again, but I heard that he survived the occupation of Berlin and lived on into his seventies. I like to think of him trying to scrape a living off the land, wearing second-hand clothes and dead men's shoes, digging up his neat lawn with its perfect stripes to grow potatoes and cabbages, keeping rabbits and chickens for food, foraging for bits of coal along the railway tracks. He died in some woman's bed. She wrote to tell me, but by the time the letter finally reached me he'd long been buried. So I never had the chance to dance on his grave, as I'd so often wished as a child.

*And what happened after your mother died?*

(LONG SILENCE)

This and that.

*Do you want to be more specific?*

The desk sergeant I used to report to was a friendly man. He let it slip that if I managed to find a job somewhere, he wouldn't ask too many questions or bother with the paperwork. There were lots of jobs advertised at that time; so many housemaids had gone off to work for the Canadians. They lived just outside Amsterdam, the Gronewegs. He owned a textile factory. The wife was some kind of invalid – or at least she liked to take to her bed when the mood took her – and, as they entertained a lot, they needed help with the cooking and serving and looking after the children. 'We don't care where you've come from, or what you did in your last job, just so long as you don't steal from us,' she told me – Mrs Groneweg – when she gave me my uniform and showed me to my little room in the attic. It felt like a palace to me after the stifling atmosphere in my grandmother's house.

*How long were you there?*

A year – no, nearly two. Then one evening, when I was serving at a cocktail party, one of the guests followed me into the kitchen. He was a bit drunk and I thought I'd have to humour him, let him try to kiss me – the guests often tipped very generously – and then get out of the kitchen fast before things went too far, but he just stood there asking me why I was working as a maid when I was so clearly very well-educated and capable of much more than domestic service. At first I thought this was some kind of chat-up line but then he went on to say that he'd tried to find out about me from his host, who had claimed to know absolutely nothing about me, not even where I came from. I told him that my studies had been interrupted. 'So what are you good at?' he asked. And, you know, I'd never really thought about it. Not for a long time, at least. I didn't know what to say. Good at walking through forests at night, trying not to jump out of my skin every time a branch snapped. Good at hiding from Russians. At sleeping in pigsties. At biting. Hard. At grieving for my mother. At living with a mouth full of teeth that hurt and moved whenever I ate anything.

*So what did you say?*

I told him I was good at languages. That I spoke fluent German and English. He winced when I said German and I thought maybe I'd made a mistake to admit it. But then he said that might be my way out of domestic service. There was a lot of coming and going since the war, he told me. Interpreters were needed everywhere.

*Didn't you have to have some kind of qualification?*

There was no shortage of people who could produce a certificate or diploma in exchange for some jars of lentils or a smoked ham, and I had the keys to the Gronewegs' larder. They couldn't understand why I wouldn't accept my final week's salary.

*And then?*

In Germany, they despised me as a cheese head. In Holland they hated me for being a German. I crossed the Channel to England in 1949 and overnight I became the nicest person in the world. And what had changed about me? Absolutely nothing. 'Oh – you're from Holland! How interesting! We love the Dutch. We went to the bulb fields once, before the war. What a wonderful sight! Rows and rows of yellow and red. What do you do? Oh, you're an interpreter. How *very* useful! *Do* come for supper.'

# Chapter Fifteen

I sit on a chair by the window, Angie's copy of the magazine in my hand. I thumb through the pages until I reach the one I'm looking for. To the right of the introduction is a photograph of Max and Susanna playing violin and flute together. Susanna looks about twelve. Behind them, a couple of teenage boys and a large dog are sprawled on an ancient, sagging, sofa. A toddler is sitting at Max's feet, clutching a piece of cloth to her face and sucking her thumb. I wonder who took the photograph and why the journalist chose this one. What he thinks it says about Max and Susanna. About childhood. About families. About me.

'Since when have I wanted the details of my life splashed all over the papers?' I said to Max on the phone the day the piece was published.

'It's one article. It's not splashed anywhere.'

'It's in the colour supplement of a national newspaper. If that's not splashed, I don't know what is.'

'You've spent your whole working life writing about other people's lives, Julia. Listening in to other people's conversations; sharing their most intimate moments. You've made a very successful career out of it.'

'That's not the same at all.'

'Isn't it?'

'No, it isn't.'

'Does Susanna know how upset you are?'

'Of course she doesn't. And don't you tell her.'

'So much for absolute truth and honesty. Have you revised your manifesto?'

'Oh, hah bloody hah.'

'I don't understand what you are so unhappy about. The article is about something that worked out really well.'

'Just look at it. It sounds like it's about a mother who is so awful that her daughter would prefer to travel thousands of miles to live with her bloody uncle than stay with her.'

'It doesn't at all.'

'Yes, it does.'

'Have you even read the thing?'

'Not beyond the first page, no. And I'm not going to.'

'Well, it doesn't say anything like that. Quite the opposite, in fact.'

'So you say.'

'You really should read the whole thing. I think you'd like it. I think you'd be pleased.'

'Yeah, well – '

'Come and see me, Julia. I miss you.'

'No way!'

'Mikey's being released on licence and is coming to stay for a bit. He's managed to track down Max-son-of-Max to an animal rescue place so they'll both be here. I'm told he's fully house-trained – Max-son-of-Max. Can't vouch for Mikey, though.'

'You really know how to show a girl a good time.'

'Come on. Come and stay. It's been ages.'

'I'll think about it.'

'Say you'll come.'

'OK. Soon. But only if you promise not to get your violin out. Or mention the sodding article.'

I look out over the green then take a deep breath and turn the page.

# < relatively*speaking*

I used to visit my grandmother every year or so from when I was about seven. We'd wait for a postcard with her address on it and then my mum would take me to England and put me on a plane to wherever my grandmother was living. It was a lot easier seeing her once I moved to England. All she carries with her is one suitcase with a few clothes in it. And a wooden angel which she hangs on the wall wherever she lives. We used to have this game where I'd rush in and see how long it took me to find where she'd hung up her angel. Once she hung it above my bed and I was so pleased I literally couldn't speak. We used to sew together, my grandmother and me. I'd bring cloth over from West Africa and we'd make it into dresses and shirts and skirts. I'm sure it's from her I got my love of material and making things. And I'm sure that's why I chose to study textiles. I loved those visits to my grandmother. I still do.

Max is about the kindest person you could meet. He fostered difficult kids for a long time – kids everyone else had given up on. And, though it didn't always work out, he never became cynical or lost his belief that everyone is basically good. That everyone has the potential for goodness within them whatever has happened to them or whatever they've done. One of the boys he'd looked after from the age of about 13 to 17 went to prison – for some quite serious offence – but he always stayed in contact with Max. He even named his terrier after him. Max never really talks about families or communities but he has always lived as part of one. People don't need to be related to him or tell him their darkest secrets to be part of his family. Max was brilliant to grow up with. I owe him so much. I can't imagine not having him in my life. I think it's a shame he never had any children of his own, but in a selfish way I'm really glad that he didn't.

## *Max Rosenthal:*

I remember Susanna visiting me in Dorset when she was about four or five. It was a really cold winter and I'm sure she'd never seen snow and ice but she was remarkably unfazed by it. She had this little child's face and body and then she would suddenly come out with something so incredibly grown-up that it would take your breath away. I suppose it was because she spent so much time just with my sister, Julia. Susanna has always been unbelievably confident and sure of herself – so different from me and Julia when we were children

– but never in a bad way. Susanna assumes that people will love her and so they do. It sounds very simple but I think it's a gift.

I have felt extraordinarily connected to Susanna since the moment I first met her. Before, even. When Julia first told me she was pregnant, I remember feeling the baby kick and knowing I'd love it. There didn't seem to be any way I couldn't love my sister's child when I loved my sister so much. I did have some misgivings. Julia was very young and was insistent that she was going to bring up her child alone in very rural parts of Africa, but she was absolutely determined and she did a great job.

> *" Susanna assumes that people will love her and so they do. "*

I knew Susanna had taken up the flute when she was six or seven and was being taught by a Catholic missionary priest, but I'd no idea how good she was. The first time she played to me, I was literally dumbstruck. I'd played the violin as a child and been pretty good at the time, but I hadn't played a note since I was about 17 or 18. I'd never had the slightest urge to even pick up an instrument, but when I heard Susanna play I borrowed a violin and, though it wasn't quite like riding a bicycle, I found I could still play reasonably well and I rediscovered my love of music

and the violin. This Steiner school has a really strong musical tradition and Susanna just got better and better. It takes arts and crafts very seriously as well, so she spent a lot of time making collages and clothes. I wasn't surprised when she chose textiles over music. She could easily have studied languages too. I can't think where she got that skill from. My grandmother Clara was German but she never spoke German to us, and Julia and I never got beyond O-level French. But when Susanna came to the Steiner school, it only took her a couple of months to catch up with her classmates who'd been learning German for five years.

I know that Julia was devastated when Susanna chose to come and live here with me. She saw it as a sign that she'd failed as a mother, when actually I think it was a sign that she'd succeeded and done a really good job. She'd produced a child who, at eleven, knew exactly what it was she needed and wasn't afraid to demand it. Susanna didn't worry that Julia would fall apart because she knew that Julia was incredibly strong, and it is Julia's strength which has allowed Susanna to become the remarkable, independent young woman she is now.

# XV

'We love the Dutch,' they all said. 'Come and stay for the weekend.' 'Let us show you around London.' 'Have you been to the Tower of London yet? To Big Ben? To Windsor Castle? Come with us, we'll take you.' 'Come for supper – we're just off the King's Road.' 'My father's got a boat on Lake Windermere – you must come sailing.' 'Yes, we love the Dutch. And what a marvellous English accent you have,' everyone said. And gradually people forgot where I was from. They didn't even hear any more that I wasn't English.

*Were you happy?*

Happy? Very. I had nothing. The contents of one small suitcase. I lived in one rented room. I had a bed, a table, a cupboard and an electric hotplate. There was a bathroom two floors up. My landlady lived below me. In the winter I could either get the bus home from work or put money in the gas meter. Sometimes all I had to eat all day was a tin of baked beans. But I was happier than I'd been for years.

*Were you lonely?*

I told you, everyone loved this girl from Holland. Especially Andrew.

*Andrew?*

His father ran the translation and interpreting service I worked for. We met outside his father's office. He'd just come down from Cambridge. I remember thinking that was a strange expression, to 'come down' from Cambridge.

*Tell me about him.*

He wasn't important.

*I'm interested.*

He was tall and slim and very good-looking. And funny, I realised, once I got used to his sense of humour. And very English. And very wealthy. And such an enthusiast! He had a private pilot's licence and used to fly me to France for the day. I hate flying now but I loved it then. He found out I was from Amsterdam and was intrigued. He thought I was the most fascinating person he'd ever met. He wanted to know all about my family and what it was like living in Holland during the war. He kept suggesting we fly there so that he could see all my old haunts, get to know some of my friends.

*Did you tell him?*

That actually I'd grown up in Berlin? That I was one of the enemy? What do you think? London was still full of bomb sites. And then he introduced me to his family and they were friendly and interested in me and Andrew's sister told me how good I was for him. That we'd be perfect together. And then he proposed to me.

*And did you accept?*

Are you mad? How could I?

*Why not?*

If you're asking that, I've been wasting my time here.

*Why couldn't you marry him?*

(SILENCE)

*Did you think you didn't deserve him?*

(SILENCE)

*Did you think you didn't deserve to be loved?*

(SILENCE)

*Did you feel you had to be punished?*

(SILENCE)

*What do you think you had to be punished for?*

(SILENCE)

# Chapter Sixteen

I hear a key in the door and then a voice calling out, 'Hello, Julia. Are you still there?'

'I'm up here.'

I slide the magazine into the middle of the pile, shut Angie's bedroom door and go downstairs.

'Had a good look around?' Angie asks pleasantly. She is putting a couple of pizzas in the oven and a box of chips into the microwave. Three girls and Ben are hovering around her. She gestures at the cardboard packaging. 'I know, it's terrible, but Fridays are a nightmare. It's a ridiculously early tea and then swimming, samba band and Guides all in different places. I should probably have spent the morning preparing a nutritious vegetable casserole but I'd end up throwing most of it in the bin – or what's left of it after they've all picked out whichever bits of vegetable they claim they're allergic to this week – so it makes more sense to go to the gym instead and feed them junk food. That way we're all happy.'

The girls – I realise that Anna and Eleanor are twins – seem only mildly surprised to have had a stranger spending the afternoon looking round their house. Their uniform – grey skirts, white shirts, maroon jumpers – is oddly familiar.

'Julia was at the same school as me and Auntie Becky. At *your* school. But the old one by the station – before they moved it. She used to live in this house a long time ago, when she was a little girl.'

'Cool. Which room did you have?' asks Catherine.

'Yours.'

'The best one!' She grins.

'I used to think so too,' I say.

'Did you like *my* room,' asks Ben hopefully.

'I did. And what a lot of guns.'

'I warned you,' laughs Angie.

'I bet you never had to share,' says Anna or Eleanor, resentfully.

'I only had a brother. So we had a room each.'

'Lucky you!'

'A nice brother?' asks Ben.

'He was. Lovely.'

'Is he dead?'

'Dead? No.'

''Cos you said *was*, which is in the past.'

'No, he's alive. Very much so. I'm going to stay with him for a few days after I leave here. He lives in Dorset now. In the middle of the countryside.'

'Did he go to *my* school?'

'No, he went on a train to his.'

'By himself?'

'Yes, all by himself.'

'Here, wash your hands, everyone,' says Angie. 'And Julia, would you like pizza and chips with this lot or a nice quiet G&T? Actually I'm not going to give you the choice. Let's leave them to it. Anna and Ellie, can you set the table and Catherine, you get the chips out of the microwave when it pings? The pizza will need a bit longer.'

Angie leads me into the sitting room and gets a bottle of gin out of a corner cabinet.

'Actually, I'd better not,' I say, sitting down. 'I'm driving.'

'Of course you are! I forgot. And so am I. Damn! What time's your appointment with the solicitor?'

'Four-thirty.' I look at my watch. It is quarter past four. 'I'd better go, I suppose.'

'Gosh, yes!' Angie says, glancing at the clock on the mantelpiece. 'What a shame. I wanted to hear all about your daughter. Do you know the way?'

'It's in Brading Road – just next to our school.'

'Where our school *used* to be, you mean! You won't recognise anything around there – it's all been pulled down and rebuilt.'

She puts the bottle of gin on the table and, rather reluctantly, shows me to the front door.

'Listen, it's been *so* lovely meeting you. Come again any time.'

'I will.'

But I know I won't.

'Thank you *so* much, Angie. For letting me look around.'

'It's a pleasure. I mean it – come back any time.'

I rehearse the journey to Brading Road as I get into the car. Left out of the Close, down the street and out of the estate, across the main road that our mother dreaded so much, past the rows of pebbledashed villas and an ugly Catholic church, and across another road to the station. Here Max and I would part company and he'd get on the train while I'd walk down the hill to my school. Between the station and school was a depot where freshly slaughtered pigs were skinned, frozen and hung upside down on great metal hooks. Racks and racks of them staring out at us, their mouths and eyes wide open. Men in white coats smeared with blood, and white peaked caps, would stand, balancing solid pigs' carcasses on their shoulders, whistling and calling out at us, and sometimes tossing a pig's penis or hairy ear in our direction. We trod carefully through the bloody debris in our outdoor shoes and ignored the rude men as our headmistress had advised us to. There would be complaints nowadays. Traumatised vegetarian schoolgirls, and their outraged parents, demanding compensation.

Angie was right. I don't recognise anything. Whole streets have disappeared. Where once there was a row of shops and a recreation ground, there is now a series of roundabouts. I head for the station, which thankfully has been allowed to remain in the same place, though the road leading down the hill has gone, along with the pig works and the school and the rows of dusty elm trees. They have been replaced by a massive shopping mall, all brick and chrome and glass. A glass lift on the outside of the building transports shoppers from one ornamental palm-infested floor to the next.

Groups of schoolchildren in black trousers and green polo shirts are hanging around at the entrance, talking on their mobile phones, eating chips, laughing. A tall, very thin girl with long, dead-straight fair hair is pinned against one of the glass doors, her hands up the shirt of a slightly shorter boy who has abandoned his sports bag a few feet away and – legs splayed for better balance – is kissing her as though he hasn't had a decent meal in days. I'd like to go up to them and say, *We weren't allowed to eat in the street in school uniform, or talk to boys anywhere near the school building, or loosen our ties, or take off our hats, let alone snog!* And no doubt they'd look at me with the same withering indifference with which they regard the mothers with pushchairs and the old people with walking sticks who are trying to negotiate a clear route round their legs and bags and chip wrappers, or the young security guard with his walkie-talkie who seems to be trying to suggest that they might like to congregate away from the shopping centre.

Somewhere around here was the first pizzeria to come to town. My friends and I thought it was unbelievably glamorous and cosmopolitan. The waiters wore very tight black trousers and even tighter black shirts, and spoke in accents that swung wildly from south London to somewhere indeterminate south of Calais. It was there that Caroline Statham once, to my surprise, invited me for a pizza after school. Always the first – to kiss with tongues, to put her hand right inside a boy's Y-fronts, and finally (so she coolly claimed, though none of us really believed her) to have full-blown sex with the man with the shaven head and the anchor tattoo who sold flowers outside the station – Caroline shared something of the glamour of the pizzeria.

'Couldn't you just tell Max?' Caroline asked me, picking off pieces of mushroom and onion and kernels of sweetcorn until all that was left of her pizza was an orangey-red spongey mass.

'Tell him what?'

'That I really fancy him.'

'Don't you think that would sound a bit weird, coming from me? Why don't you tell him yourself?'

'I don't see him on the way home any more.'

'He's doing his exams. He doesn't have to go into school very often these days. You could ring him up when you get home.'

'I can't do that. He'll think I'm some kind of slag. And anyway, your dad's really scary.'

'He's not scary.'

'Well, he sounds pretty scary on the phone.'

'He's just tired.'

'What's he doing at home so early in the afternoon, anyway? I thought he was some kind of "famous doctor".' Caroline drew little inverted commas in the air with her fingers.

'He's been ill.'

'Shouldn't he be able to cure himself? If he's such a "famous doctor"?' she asked, her greasy fingers repeating the punctuation marks.

I watched, hating her, as she took a bite of pizza. A long thread of pinkish cheese stuck to the side of her face and hung forlornly from her chin.

'Do you think Max *would* go out with me?'

'I don't know. He doesn't really go out with anyone.'

'Well, that's a lie. I've seen him out with loads of different girls.'

'He doesn't want that kind of relationship. He told me.'

'What kind of relationship?'

'I don't know. You'll have to ask him.'

'Don't just say things and then not be able to explain them. That's pathetic. Look, I paid for your pizza.'

'I know. Thanks. It was nice.'

'So now you have to ask him.'

'Okay, I will, but I can't promise anything.'

'And don't tell him about Kevin-at-the-flower-stall. I don't want him to get the wrong idea about me. We didn't really go all the way.'

Max smiled as I told him about the pizza outing and passed on the message.

'So what shall I tell her, Max?'

'That next time you'll have the pepperoni.'

'Ha bloody ha. What shall I really tell her?'

'That I'll be going away very soon, so it's probably not the best time to start a relationship.'

'I'm not sure it's a relationship she wants. More like your body. God knows why.'

'Oh, well, in that case just give me her number.'

'You don't mean that.'

'No, I don't mean that. I'm going to be pretty busy at the hostel from what I've read about it. And it's very much men only.'

'Don't go.'

'I have to. I've accepted the job.'

'You're not even being paid.'

'That's not the point.'

'Exactly. There's no point. Stay here.'

'I can't. I really want to go.'

'But what about me?'

'You'll be fine. You've got loads of friends – and anyway, you'll be gone in a couple of years. There'll be no stopping you.'

'You can't leave me here with Mum and Dad. I'll die.'

'Don't you think you're being a teeny bit melodramatic?'

'OK, I won't die, but it'll be awful. Without you.'

'You can come and visit me. It's only north London. I'll sneak you in.'

'Do you promise?'

'But only if you don't cry.'

'I'm not crying.'

'But only if clear salty liquid doesn't come out of the little holes next to your eyes. Come here, stupid.'

Max came over to me and wrapped me in his arms. And even as I buried my face in his school shirt and wept at the thought of life at home without him, I felt a little flicker of victory. Caroline Statham would never, ever get to hold my brother this close.

# XVI

I met him at a party in Bloomsbury. Or rather I saw him there.

*Andrew?*

Not Andrew, no.

*No, sorry, of course not.*

(SILENCE)

*Go on.*

I'd come back from another long day at the agency. It was all a bit awkward there since I'd turned down Andrew's proposal. I'd had to walk as I'd spent my bus fare on a roll and a piece of cheese – and I was pretty tired and hungry. I couldn't afford to put any more money in the gas meter, so, when the girl in the room above mine invited me to her boyfriend's party, a hot, crowded room with free food seemed a good idea. It's odd how clearly I remember that party. I asked the girl, 'Who's that little man on his own, over there by the window?' And she said something like, 'Oh that's Oscar Rosenthal. He's a doctor. Frightfully clever, John says.' She couldn't remember how her boyfriend knew him. She'd met him once or twice before – but he was a bit of a dark horse. She thought maybe I could get something out of him. 'You're the interpreter,' she said. But by the time we'd pushed our way through the crowd, he'd left.

194

*And then...*

And then a few weeks after that, late one Friday afternoon, I was called in to the casualty department of the local hospital to translate for an elderly man who had been found lying on his floor at home. He was thin and confused but pretty strong for someone who hadn't eaten for a few days, and there was no way he was going to let anyone in a uniform near him. He was sitting up in the bed and shouting at the nurses in a mixture of Yiddish and German. And I went up to him and put my hand on his shoulder and told him in German, 'It's all right. You're quite safe here. You're in a hospital in London. No one is going to hurt you. They just want to put in a drip – it's just saline. Salt water. It'll make you feel a lot better. I'll stay here with you and keep an eye on them while they do it.' And he looked up at me and smiled very weakly and stretched out his arm and I noticed that he had blue numbers tattooed on it. And when the doctor came to take his arm, and put in the drip, I saw that it was the same quiet little man from the party. (SILENCE) And somehow we ended up having a cup of coffee in the doctor's mess, the little doctor and me. I liked his stillness. And I liked the way he didn't say very much and his lack of that very English skill of small talk. I liked the way he didn't ask me lots of questions about myself like all the others did. And he had kind eyes. And then he looked at his watch and asked me if I'd like a glass of sherry. He had a bottle in his room that a patient had given him. And I liked the way it took him a couple of cigarettes and a glass of sherry and a couple of false starts to ask me if I'd like to go to a Prom with him the next week. He said he had a spare ticket and it would be a shame to let it go to waste. But if I didn't want to come, it didn't matter at all. He wasn't even sure he wouldn't be on call that evening. So different from Andrew with his very English confidence and his certainty that there was nothing I could possibly want to do other than spend every minute of the day with him. I liked this quiet little man's voice, with its almost imperceptible trace of an accent. I liked the way he occupied the room but still didn't really seem to fit in. That there was something of the foreigner about him. Something of the outsider. 'All right,' I said. 'I'd love to.' We did go to the Prom and then he walked me back to my room. I could see the landlady's curtains twitch as we stood together outside the house. He told me he had a new job beginning the following week, in Newcastle. A six-month contract and then he hoped he'd be back in London to start a job in paediatrics. If I was still here when he got back, he'd rather like to see me again. But, of course, only if I had nothing better to do. He took my landlady's phone number. I didn't really expect to hear from him again. And life went on very much as before. But almost exactly six months later the phone rang and it was him. I was surprised at how pleased I was to hear his voice. Once, months later, we were in Hyde Park and there were all these couples laughing and holding hands, and old men on their soapboxes ranting about the government or rationing or whatever – just saying whatever came into their heads – and I said to Oscar, 'This could never have happened where I come from. Do you even know where that is? There's so much we don't know about each other – so much about the past – my past.' And he said, 'Why should I be interested in the past? Why should the past matter?' And he just smiled his shy smile. And that was that. No past. Just a future. And then it was New Year's Eve and he asked me if I'd spend it with him. He'd like to take me to Trafalgar Square. And as we stood by the fountain, as the chimes of Big Ben rang out and everyone shouted and cheered, he took my hand and asked me to marry him. And I thought, yes, why not? Maybe this is someone I could be happy with. Maybe this is someone I could make happy. Maybe this is the future.

# Chapter Seventeen

Brading Road has somehow survived the years of relentless redevelopment. Farrer & Farrer is housed in what must have been quite a large Edwardian family villa. The name is stencilled across the windows of the ground floor. A plump woman in her thirties, wearing a paisley patterned blouse and plain navy skirt, looks up at me expectantly. Her expensively highlighted hair is scraped off her face and secured with a navy velvet Alice band.

'It's Rosenthal. Julia Rosenthal,' I say. 'I've got an appointment at four-thirty.'

'Bear with me a moment.'

She flicks through her appointment book, then glances at her watch and frowns slightly. 'Ah, yes. With Mr Blenkinsop. I'll see if he's still here.'

'I think the name on the letter was Turner.'

'Mr Turner's on holiday this week, I'm afraid. Mr Blenkinsop is handling his clients.'

She presses a button on her phone.

'Nigel. Your client is here now. Yes, your four-thirty. Yes, I know it is. Shall I send her through? OK, no problem.'

She looks up at me and smiles tightly. 'Do take a seat, Mrs Rosenthal. Mr Blenkinsop will be with you shortly.'

'Thank you. Actually, it's not Mrs Rosenthal.'

'I'm sorry?'

'Mrs Rosenthal is my mother. That's why I'm here. It's Dr, if you need a title.'

The receptionist looks down at her appointment book. Her cheeks are flushed with irritation.

The phone rings. She picks it up.

'The key to which cupboard, Nigel? It's in the safe.' She laughs, coyly. 'I don't know where you'd be without me either!'

I pick up a brochure from the table. Whoever Farrer & Farrer once were, they've been replaced by David Turner, Nigel Blenkinsop and Jonathan Markham, all three of whom smile up at me in their sensible dark suits and ties that have been chosen to suggest just a hint of fun. From one of Angie's catalogues, probably. I stare at the picture of Nigel Blenkinsop. He is slightly overweight. What little is left of his hair has been cut very short. His eyes are blue. *Trust me, they say. Make me the executor of your will. Let me do your conveyancing. Have this dance with me.*

And Nigel Blenkinsop takes Katie Powell's hand and leads her, in her dark blue Laura Ashley maxi-dress with the Chinese collar, away from the table, sticky with Coke and lemonade and soggy Cheezy Footballs and Twiglets, and on to the dance floor. And as their faces flash green, red and blue, and silver slivers of light flicker across the ceiling, my heart breaks into a thousand tiny pieces.

The phone rings again.

'OK, Nigel, I'll send *Dr* Rosenthal in.'

She looks up at me, unsmiling. 'If you'd like to go through now. Second door on the right.'

Nigel Blenkinsop leans over his desk to shake my hand.

'I think we've met before,' I say.

'Have we?' He smiles, questioningly. 'Do sit down.'

'Thanks. In about 1973. Weren't you at St Peter's?'

'I was. For my sins.'

'Do you remember the discos – with the girls from the High School?'

He grimaces. 'How could I forget?'

'I used to go to them with my best friend, Katie Powell. Actually, she wasn't my best friend for long.'

For one awful moment, I think he is going to say, *You mean my lovely wife Katie*, but he continues to look blank.

'Never mind,' I say. 'It was a very long time ago. I wouldn't really expect you to remember.'

'I suppose I had hair then.' He smiles, brushing his hand across his head. I notice he has a tiny hole in one earlobe. And a chunky silver ring on the wedding finger of his right hand. Clearly Farrer & Farrer's dress code, while embracing the jaunty tie, stops short at any overt indication of homosexuality.

'You did – lots of it. I think it was the Noddy Holder look you were cultivating at the time.'

'Oh, well.' He smiles again, ruefully. 'Back to business.'

He puts his hand on a box that is sitting on his desk. It is a little smaller than a shoebox and wrapped in brown paper. The string is sealed with hard red wax.

'Your mother deposited this box with Farrer & Farrer many years ago. Around the time the firm helped her with the sale of her property. We had instructions, in the event of her death, to contact you or your brother and hand it over.'

'But she's not dead.'

'So I understand from her recent correspondence with the firm. And in good health, I hope?

'Very. She's walking in Germany at the moment. She wanted to spend her birthday there.'

'Well, that's different! My mother celebrated her last birthday in that old Aberdeen Steak House at the edge of the Mall. She's very much of the "I'm not all that keen on foreign food" generation. Luckily she doesn't seem to have noticed that Scotland's gone independent. So, as I was saying, David Turner received a new instruction recently, asking us to carry out her wishes now, rather than after her death.'

'Do you know why she changed her mind?'

'No – we rather thought you might.'

'I've no idea.'

'Ah, well. Families, eh? Thirty years in this business and I've stopped being surprised about anything very much. There's just a bit of paperwork to sort out. I thought I had the forms here but I must have left them in David Turner's office. I'm really sorry about that. I'll just be a couple of minutes.'

I try to imagine my mother getting into her car and driving to Farrer & Farrer to deposit the box. I wonder what she was wearing – what she was thinking. I wonder if it was the last thing she did before she locked up the house and left the Close for the last time.

For about a year after my father died, she stayed in Tenterden Close. I never saw her leave the house, though I suppose she must have done from time to time. As I came and went during my year between school and university, in which I did very little, I'd sometimes catch sight of her sitting in his chair in the study, gazing out at the garden, or lying on her bed, staring up at the ceiling. She didn't say much during those months. Once when I came home, I saw that she had taken all her clothes out of her cupboards and was stuffing them into black dustbin liners. I stopped counting when I reached twenty-five.

'What are you going to do with them?' I asked.

'I'm giving most of them away. Max put me in touch with an organisation that'll take them. If you want anything, help yourself, but it'll have to be today. The bags are being collected in the morning.'

Then one day, she invited Max and me for supper and told us that she had sold the house and bought a small flat in central London. We would be welcome to stay there whenever we wanted to. She would put our stuff in storage and we could get it out when we had somewhere to put it. The flat would be her base too, but she didn't think she would be there much. She would sell it as soon as we didn't need it any more.

'Where are you going?' we asked.

'I'm not sure yet – I just know that I'm going.'

And that's what she did. She went. Travelling everywhere by train or boat. Carrying one small suitcase. I think she was the owner of a capsule wardrobe before the term was ever invented. For the last thirty years or so she has lived in France, the Czech Republic, Spain, Italy, Switzerland, Portugal and Morocco. Sometimes in large cities, sometimes in the countryside; sometimes moving on after only a few months, sometimes staying in the same place for a couple of years. Once, only once, my mother travelled by air. She flew out to Cameroon just after Susanna was born. I remember how she picked up my tiny baby and whispered in her ear, 'You see, I kept my promise. I said I'd visit her *wherever* she went to live.' I had to leave the room so that she wouldn't see me cry.

My mother keeps in touch by postcard, even though she's got a laptop and is very comfortable with modern communications technology. Whenever Max or I visit her, she is pleased to see us but seems quite relieved when it's time for us to go and she can revert to her solitary life. She appears to be on nodding terms with her neighbours, but we are never introduced. The one person whose company she seems to really enjoy, whom she doesn't seem at all keen to get rid of, is Susanna. It was Susanna who once told me that she and her grandmother had bumped into a gentleman in the entrance hall of the apartment in Paris who addressed my mother as Mrs Evans and made some allusion to her former career in the Foreign Office. In Prague, it appeared that my mother was a retired headmistress from Hampshire. When I told Max, he just shrugged his shoulders and smiled.

My mother always hated her birthdays and would usually be out of contact as the date approached, so Max and I were surprised when she wrote us identical postcards informing us that she would be celebrating her birthday in Berlin and was then going to spend a few weeks walking. There was a particular forest route she wanted to retrace. Susanna had kindly agreed to accompany her.

'Retrace? I didn't know she'd ever been to Germany,' I said to Max on the phone. 'And why Berlin of all places, for her birthday?'

'Why not? It's supposed to be quite an amazing city these days. I read a really interesting article about the new Reichstag. I'd love to go.'

'But since when has she "celebrated" a birthday? She could barely tolerate all the birthdays we spent with her.'

'I know! Remember the miserable fortieth?'

'I've tried to eradicate it from my memory. And what forest route? How far can an eighty-three-year-old walk, for God's sake?'

'I imagine that this eighty-three-year-old can walk a pretty long way. Probably further than Susanna.'

'And why did Mum invite Susanna along and not us?'

'Maybe she wanted an interpreter? Susanna's German's pretty fluent.'

'And walking's never exactly been her thing. Either of their things. And why didn't Susanna tell me she was going? It must all have been arranged when I last spoke to her. When she rang me about that article.'

'After all these years, you're still asking questions that you're never going to get any answers to. Stop wondering and come and spend a few days with me. With me and Max-son-of-Max. Mikey's back inside. Come on, Julia. I really want to see you.'

So that's what my mother is doing now. Walking through the forests of Germany with my daughter as I sit here in Farrer & Farrer, looking at a small box on the solicitor's desk.

'So sorry to have kept you,' says Nigel Blenkinsop, coming into the room clutching a few sheets of paper. 'So, I'll just need a couple of signatures. Here… and here… and here. Lovely. Thanks. That all seems to be in order. Perhaps we'll meet again some time,' he says without a lot of conviction.

He shakes my hand and passes me the box. It isn't heavy – about the weight of a couple of hardback books. The receptionist is standing at the front door, a bunch of keys in her hands. Very slowly – so that she can be sure that I realise that the office is now closed and she has had to stay late on a Friday evening – she unlocks the door.

I get into the car. I look at the package. It's addressed to the two of us, to Max and me. I wonder for a moment whether to wait until I get to Max's house before I open it, then I break the seal and pull off the string and brown paper. Inside the cardboard box is a set of cassettes. They are numbered one to sixteen, but, apart from that, there is nothing to suggest what they contain. I pick out the first one and insert it into the cassette player. Then I start the ignition, press *play* and set off.

# I

(LONG SILENCE)

*So?*

So what?

*Shall we begin?*

Begin where?

*Anywhere you like.*

Is that all you're going to say?

*For now.*

And is that supposed to be helpful?

*I hope so.*

I don't know where to begin.

*You'll know. Just take your time.*

You would say that. Time is money. Isn't that the expression?

*Just take your time.*

(SILENCE)

I don't know where to begin. You'll have to give me some kind of clue. Some idea. Or is that against the rules?

*There aren't those sorts of rules.*

That's what you say.

*Well, what about beginning with a memory? Your earliest memory, perhaps.*

What are you expecting? Me floating about in the womb? The swish of warm amniotic fluid? The reassuring sound of my mother's heartbeat? The feeling of utter calm before the storm of birth? Isn't that the kind of thing you people are interested in? Or some kind of strange recurring dream in which I kill my mother and sleep with my father?

*I don't think we need be that ambitious.*

Do you think this is funny?

*Not at all. Do you?*

## Acknowledgements

*Interpreters* was inspired by a journey I made to Germany for the eightieth birthday celebrations of an old family friend. On returning to England, I knew I wanted to write about the experience of being a middle-class child of immigrant parents and the degree to which we are defined by, and interpret, our upbringing. Above all, I wanted to explore the changing experience of childhood – particularly a 1970s childhood, when children were largely excluded from the complexities of adult life and when there was no sense of entitlement to an explanation of, or information about, their parents' lives. I wanted, too, to better understand the experience of growing up so close to the Second World War, to recognise the wish of many people to place a distance between their present and that particular element of their pasts. And to explore the ambiguities of young, ordinary people who grew up in Germany in the 1930s and 1940s feeling, decades later, a requirement upon them to share in an experience of collective shame.

During the years that I have spent thinking about the ethical issues inherent in writing memoir and autobiography, while working on a PhD in creative writing at the University of Sussex, I have come to share something of Lily Briscoe's belief, in *To the Lighthouse*, that we can never really know the truth about anyone or any event, that 'this making up scenes about them, is what we call "knowing" people, "thinking" of them, "being fond" of them! Not a word of it [is] true...'. Increasingly I have come to believe that if one can never really know the truth, even about those closest to us, it would be more ethical, even more 'true', to fictionalise whatever truths we think we know.

In *Interpreters*, I have attempted to retain the emotional core of my childhood and a few key facts. I am indebted to my indomitable grandmother's memoirs of her years in Turkey, on which I have drawn quite heavily. Beyond this, *Interpreters* is a work of fiction. But there are some emotional truths within that fiction. Like Julia, I wish I had known my father better and for longer. Max was inspired by the very precious relationship I have with my two brothers (neither of whom is a free-spirited, blond-haired Steiner school teacher, artist or foster-carer). Julia's mother is a product of my imagination but very much inspired by the love, respect and gratitude I feel for my own mother.

I am grateful to my husband, Alastair, and my children, Anna and Sebastian, for their unstinting love and support. Bobbie Farsides and Bruce Young were hugely encouraging at the start of my writing career and continue to be so. Many thanks, too, for their support and encouragement in so very many ways, to Lee-Anne Mason, Kate Whyman, Martha Leyton, Martin Shovel, Sarah Mistry, Paul Keyte, Margaretta Jolly and Sue Roe. I am indebted to Candida Lacey and to Vicky Blunden, Linda McQueen and all at Myriad Editions for their support, belief and editorial suggestions. I am grateful, too, to my colleagues and students at Brighton and Sussex Medical School for the most stimulating and enjoyable 'day job' anyone could wish for. And thanks to Arts Council England for the Grant for the Arts that bought me some writing time in the tranquil silence of St Cuthman's Retreat Centre.

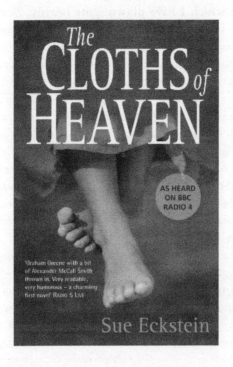

If you liked *Interpreters*, you might like Sue Eckstein's critically acclaimed début novel *The Cloths of Heaven*.

For an exclusive extract, read on...

Daniel squeezed his way along the narrow paths of the market, his face brushing against the warm round backs of babies tied tightly to the women who strolled between the stalls, balancing containers of cooking oil, or flimsy red and white striped plastic bags of vegetables, on their heads. He breathed in the milky, tinny smell of the sleeping babies, the odour of rotting cabbage and kola nut spittle mingled with smoked fish and musty rice.

'Come here, sir – nice things.'

'Bananas – very cheap – come, come.'

'Any pens? Any bonbons?'

'New videos, no pirates, come, buy.'

'Give me one lamasi…'

The shouts of traders competing for business, the sound of raised voices bargaining over clusters of misshapen tomatoes, the music of Bob Marley and Salif Keita blaring from the cassette-copying booths fought for space in the hot dry air. As Daniel took off his sunglasses to wipe his face, the market exploded into colour. Gleaming aluminium cooking pots and gaudy Chinese enamelware flashed in the sun, piles of aubergines glowed in a purple haze, pyramids of tinned tomato paste glinted. The cloth of the women's robes and headdresses dazzled him.

He found himself walking to the edge of the market, towards the fetid canal which flowed, sluggishly, to the port. Here the rickety kiosks selling batteries, cigarettes, and sticks of white bread gave way to larger shops, cloth warehouses and wholesalers. The vast concrete buildings stretched back from the litter-strewn, potholed pavements.

Daniel stopped outside the largest cloth shop, hesitated for a moment, then ducked under the raised grille and went in. He blinked, unable to make out anything until his eyes became accustomed to the dark interior. Fans turned above the high wooden shelves and ankle-height platforms that held the cloth. Motes of dust danced in the few rays of sun that had penetrated the half-closed shutters. The floor was concrete; bare light bulbs hung from the high ceiling. There was a tall wooden desk and chair in the corner, of the kind favoured by Dickensian bookkeepers. On top of the desk he noticed a calculator, a pile of receipts on a spike, and a novel spread face down, bursting from its spine.

He walked along the aisles, trailing his fingers across the bolts of cloth. As he did so, he could feel the textures in his teeth and on his tongue: the smooth damasks, the fuzzy appliqués, the stiff nets, the deep mauve gauze dotted with pink felt, the gold-embossed rayon trickling strands of silver thread, the lemon polyester with its universe of sparkling orange stars.

He became aware of the hum of a computer and looked up. At the far end of the shop was a glass-fronted gallery. A window had been slid open and he could hear the high-pitched whine of a fax machine. He could just make out the dark head of someone sitting in front of the computer.

He walked back along the first aisle, then stopped suddenly by one of the thick concrete columns. She was sitting at the high wooden desk, bent over the book. He wondered how she had got there without his noticing. It was the closest he had been to her. Daniel could see traces of perspiration on her forehead. From time to time, she raised a hand to push her damp hair from her face. She was wearing a simple black cotton dress. Her thin arms were bare.

'Rachel!'

She held her place in the book with a finger and looked up at the gallery.

Daniel felt his palms prick with sweat. Rachel. Surely that couldn't just be another of those coincidences?

'Rachel. Did you hear me? Has that consignment from China arrived?'

'Not yet.'

'I'm going out for a while. Deal with it when it comes, will you?'

She turned back to her book without replying.

A short, dark, immaculately dressed man walked down the wooden stairs from the gallery. He stopped by the desk, gripped her arm with one hand and turned her face to his with the other. He kissed her slowly on the lips, then let her go.

'Faysal and Suhad are coming for dinner, darling. Please be ready,' he called behind him as he left.

She wiped her mouth on the back of her hand, then flicked through the book until she found her place.

Daniel hesitated a moment, then went up to the desk. He could see the imprint of the man's fingers on her arm. He took a deep breath.

'You like Mervyn Peake, then?'

She looked up and stared at him impassively for a few seconds before returning to the book.

'I loved the first two Gormenghast books...'

Daniel stopped, unnerved by the lack of response. He felt himself blush. He could kick himself. Not only did he do a good line in wincing and looking away, he could come up with a damn fine irrelevant question.

'I've seen you a few times, here in the shop.'

'I know,' she said, without lifting her eyes from the book.

'I hope you don't think I'm – '

'Do you want to buy some cloth?' She shut the book and stared at him.

'Sorry?'

'Do you want to buy some cloth? If not, I suggest – '

'Yes, I do.' Daniel scanned the rows, his eyes frantic. 'Some of the – the damask – that bright pink. The one with the fuchsia pattern in it. Three metres.'

She walked to the bolt of cloth with an elegant weariness, leaving her leather sandals under the desk.

He watched her as she dragged the bolt on to a long wooden table, measured it with a wooden ruler, snipped it with a pair of large black scissors, and then ripped the piece from the bolt. She folded the cloth, wrapped it in paper, tied the parcel with string, and handed it to him.

'That's forty lamasi. Thanks. Any more? You're obviously quite a connoisseur. What about the crimson and purple nylon over there? Or the pure cotton with repeating images of Pope John Paul II?'

Her voice was icily polite.

'No. Thanks. This is fine. I'm sorry to have – '

'The Virgin Mary on best quality polyester?' She pulled out length after length of cloth. 'We've got the Wailers around here somewhere, too. On rayon.'

'No. This is great. Look, if I've – '

'Ethnic African batik? Freshly imported from the Netherlands.'

'No, really. This is just what I wanted.'

'No, it isn't.'

'No. You're right. I just wondered who you are.'

'Who I am?'

'And what you're doing here.'

'What does it look like?' She returned to her chair and opened the book again.

'And I wanted to see if you were all right.'

'Why shouldn't I be?'

'After last night.'

She looked up at him. Her eyes were greyish-green, he noticed.

'I saw you and – and him,' Daniel nodded up at the gallery, 'on the coast road. Last night. I just wondered – '

'I'm fine,' said Rachel flatly. She took a deep breath. 'But thanks for asking.'

213

'That's OK. It's just that things seemed, sort of, well, difficult. Look, I'll give you my card. Perhaps you'd give me a ring some time. If I can do anything.'

She looked at the card. 'Yes. Thanks. I may do that. Some time.'

'Well, thanks for this,' said Daniel, as he picked up his parcel. 'Goodbye.'

He walked back out into the street and watched Rachel for a moment through the grille. He saw her look at the card again, then slowly rip it up and let the tiny pieces flutter to the floor.

She looked at the card. "Yes. Thanks. I may do that. Some

# MORE FROM MYRIAD EDITIONS

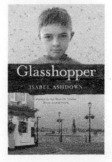